No talking now. And please, I prayed, no twig snapping. He doubled over, inched cautiously forward, barely moving. A freeze sent a chill down my spine. In the deep night silence a dog barked once, miles away, and a car rolled by on a road far behind us where my Honda stood under a beech tree. Slowly we closed the gap, and stopped.

In the glare from a floodlight on some nearby building, the fence sprang into relief against the darkness.

"It's a chain link," Brenda whispered, rasping.

I clapped a hand over her mouth. It was indeed chain link, topped by evil-looking concertina wire, and it looked at least ten feet high. What's more, there was a very alert man walking slowly back and forth behind it, with a very large, very ugly rifle in a shoulder sling. Beyond him, lined up with their noses all pointing in the same direction, sat a neat row of huge B52s, massively waiting.

C. B. GREENFIELD:
A LITTLE
MADNESS

Lucille Kallen

BALLANTINE BOOKS • NEW YORK

Library of Congress Catalog Card Number: 85-18290

ISBN 0-345-31119-1

This edition published by arrangement with Random House, Inc.

Manufactured in the United States of America

First Ballantine Books Edition: May 1987

For my son, Paul,
the unmasker of demagogues,
and my daughter, Lise,
the climber of perilous fences

ACKNOWLEDGMENTS

I must belatedly mention that in writing this and other books I have always, for the odd facts, dates, names and references that escape me, consulted my resident human encyclopedia, Herb Engel.

As for some highly specialized information in this book, I was fortunate in being able to enlist the help of Lt. Col. Myron L. Donald, USAF, who was not only tireless in answering my innumerable questions, but turned the job into a pleasure.

I owe thanks as well to D. C. Hadley, managing editor of the *Finger Lakes Times*; Assistant Chief of Police Jack de Agazio; photojournalist Jim Bradley; activists Diane Chira and LeAnne Irwin; expedition aide Joan Probber; and unfailing source Captain William E. Trefny.

A little Madness in the Spring
Is wholesome even for the King.

—EMILY DICKINSON

CHAPTER ONE

WE CREPT ALONG IN THE DARK, CROUCHING IN the tall grass through the pale patches of moonlight between the clumps of trees, making what we hoped was a beeline for the barbed-wire fence that surrounded the base. The night air was chilly after a morning of wet mist and a sunless afternoon, the damp of the wild grass and scrub was clinging to my jeans and I'd neglected to change the T-shirt under my windbreaker for something warmer. If June was bustin' out over the rest of the country, it was not yet doing so here.

Beside me, Brenda's white legs alternately crouched and stalked, apparently without benefit of feet or torso. She wore a black poncho over her shirt and shorts, and navy sneakers, in the fond belief she would be invisible in the dark. Unfortunately I could think of nothing more certain to be spotted by any man with reasonable vision than a pair of shapely female legs. And there must be a thousand men behind that fence, some of them unquestionably patrolling.

I crept on, feeling brave, anxious and ridiculous by turns, the wire clippers in my pocket bumping rhythmically against my hip. Brenda's feet, keeping pace at my side, had no talent for stealth: they were stepping on fallen twigs and snapping them, kicking up stones that knocked against other stones, and generally making what sounded to me like the noise of a battalion on the move.

"Watch it, Brenda," I murmured.

The white oval of her street-urchin face under cropped black curls peered at me through the dark. "So what do you think?" she said in a hoarse whisper. "You think all this is going to do any good?"

"I think we're better off speaking quietly," I said. "That whisper crackles like the beginning of a forest fire."

She changed to a gravelly mutter. "I don't think it's going to do any good."

"Have faith."

"That's what I don't have any of. For a person with no faith, it's amazing what I do. I think I have a sickness: show me a lost cause and I drop everything and go. I worked for Eugene McCarthy. I raised money to keep the developers from tearing down the Helen Hayes Theater. I went down to Washington and marched in front of the Capitol for fourteen hours carrying an ERA sign—you notice how impressed they were."

"The verdict isn't in on the ERA."

She nodded her head, resigned. "Anything I have a compulsion to save is doomed. That's what a compulsion is, right? You fly in the face of common sense. There's a cat where I live, it's a street cat, a Bowery cat, likes to be out and around. I found it shivering in a doorway one night in January, licking an old wine bottle sticking out of a brown paper bag. Looked to me like a lost cause, so right away I took it home, gave it some tuna casserole and milk, bought it a nice Kitty Litter. First chance it got, it took off, down four flights of stairs, out to the street, I found it at the corner of Delancey and Bowery, rubbing up against an old drunk, meowing to get at the guy's bottle. Three times I took it home, three times it ran back to the Bowery. The cat's a wino."

I put out a hand, grabbed her arm, pointed to a haze of light up ahead. We'd found a section of the perimeter fence.

No talking now. And please, I prayed, no twig snapping. We doubled over, inched cautiously forward, barely moving. A breeze sent a chill down my spine. In the deep night silence a dog barked once, miles away, and a car rolled by on a road far behind us where my Honda stood under a beech tree. Slowly we closed the gap, and stopped.

In the glare from a floodlight on some nearby building, the fence sprang into relief against the darkness.

"Shit!" Brenda whispered, rasping. "It's chain link!"

I clapped a hand over her mouth. It was indeed chain link, topped by evil-looking concertina wire, and it looked at least ten feet high. What's more, there was a very alert man walking slowly back and forth behind it, with a very large, very ugly rifle in a shoulder sling. Beyond him, lined up with their noses all pointing in the same direction, sat a neat row of huge B52s, massively waiting.

I turned Brenda's face toward me, pointed urgently in the direction from which we'd just come, and led the retreat. When we were more than halfway back to the road I stopped and waited for her to catch up.

"We could've been shot!" she gasped.

"Only if he saw us and told us to stop, and we kept coming." Deadly force was what they called it. Beyond this point illegal entry will be met by deadly force. Sheer poetry.

"Did you *see* them?" She meant the bombers.

"They're not easy to miss."

"They . . . they've got to be loaded, right?"

3

"There wouldn't be much point in sending them up empty."

She sat down suddenly, in the grass, her hands clutching her forehead. "Cruises! We were standing maybe a hundred feet from . . . from . . . I feel sick."

I didn't feel too jaunty myself. "Well, at least we know where we are. That's the Alert Area, and those planes are at one end of the runway; if we want the other end of the runway we have to go two miles . . . *that* way."

"If it's still chain link down there," she said, getting up, "I'll see you back at the ranch."

We found our way back to the car and drove down the road that followed the curve of the base property. I felt short of breath, apprehensive, and at the same time strangely removed from what I was doing. There was an unreality about all this. I could not possibly be in this upstate outpost, about to breach the boundary of a military base full of Bombardment Wings, Fighter Interceptor Squadrons, Operations Control Centers. Nothing in my background ever suggested that I would one day be sneaking through dark and unknown fields to wrestle with barbed wire, to confront military police. I led an ordinary, suburban, upper-middle-class life. Going to concerts I understood. Bloomingdale's I could cope with. Libraries, supermarkets, a garden, a typewriter, a dog: the average reasonably-well-feathered empty nest.

I read the news, I even wrote some of it. Of course I was appalled at rampant nuclear lunacy. But so was everyone I knew and valued, and *they* weren't here. *They* weren't taking illegal action, putting themselves on the line, standing up to be taken into custody, jailed, blown away, whatever happened when you tangled with implacable men in blue berets and rifle slings.

Never mind that we were not there to blow up a bridge or plant the airfield with land mines, that it was only a reconnaissance we were on, a relatively simple matter of finding the shortest route from a civilian road to a specific point inside the base, and clipping the fence so that others

4

could enter, later—it was still a hazardous mission: set one foot on the turf beyond that fence and you were in jeopardy.

Through the open car window a change in the direction of the wind brought us the faint sound of massed voices from the main gate. An hour earlier we'd passed by the gate, and seen in the stark white light of the floodlights on the guard shacks, forty or fifty women in a variety of sizes, ages and shapes, sitting cross-legged on the ground, or leaning against the fence, some of them shaking it, others tying themselves to it, all of them chanting.

Unreal, I thought. But it was real enough.

"They're supposed to be experts," Brenda complained, slouching beside me. "JoAnne and Harriet. They swore it was four-strand barbed wire once you got away from the main gate."

"It probably is. That's a top security area back there, after all. Not exactly a place for welcome mats."

The mileage indicator said we'd arrived. On one side of the road, a scattering of ordinary houses with front yards, on the other—the primrose path to eternity. I parked in front of a squat little house with a glassed-in front porch: there were two other cars on the street, unable to park in driveways already occupied. A quiet, residential neighborhood, two miles south of a batch of Air Launched Cruise Missiles and just across the street from the point of no return.

On the uninhabited side of the road a meadow of low brush and grass separated civilian land from military. We ambled along in front of the houses, two citizens out for a nighttime stroll, until we reached an empty stretch from which no casual eye behind a darkened window might catch sight of us making for the base, then crossed the road and set out across the weedy terrain. There was much less cover here, and the crouching was so continuous I began to despair of ever being able to straighten up if and when we did reach the fence.

Brenda, this time, was the one who spotted it first.

"Barbed wire!" she hissed triumphantly.

Four thorny strands of wire, a little over a foot apart, rose to about half the height of the tall fence we'd seen earlier.

We crept close, to a point where a good-sized hickory near the fence provided some camouflage, and scanned the area beyond for any sign of movement. There was none. All was dark and quiet in the warriors' encampment. Whatever was going on was invisible and inaudible. Neatly contained. Under control. Sleek. No ragged band of men grumbling around their night fires, voicing their fears, their second thoughts. No colorful criticism here of the king's strategies—none, at least, that you could hear. Aside from that, and a lot of technology, nothing basic had changed since Harry at Agincourt.

But if the cause be not good, the king himself hath a heavy reckoning to make, when all those legs and arms and heads, chopped off in a battle, shall join together at the latter day and cry all "We died at such a place."

"Okay," Brenda whispered. "Go! Do it!" I did nothing. The wire clippers hung heavily in my pocket. Clipping a government fence is punishable in federal court, I thought.

"Why don't we try stretching it apart and climbing through?" I suggested, murmuring an inch from her ear. Her eyes widened in horror. She pointed to her bare legs. Stupid kid, I thought, though she was easily thirty, couldn't wear a pair of jeans: *"They'll slow me down."*

Clenching my jaw, I took the wire cutters from my pocket, fixed them on the top strand of wire, and pressed. Nothing happened. I reversed them, used both hands, and squeezed. There was a snap like a gunshot in the silent night and the clippers fell from my nerveless hands into the grass. We froze, waiting for a searchlight to pin us in its apprehending glare, a siren to go off, a pair of beefy arms to shoot out of the dark and fasten their vise-like fingers around our arms.

Nothing stirred beyond the fence. After a minute or two, Brenda wheezed, "Come on! Go!"

"Wait." The blood was still hammering at my chest. I crouched down, searched for the clippers, couldn't find them. Just as well, I knew I could never repeat that action. Never. Nor could I stand there while Brenda did it. I motioned to her to follow and hurried, crouching, away from the fence, toward the road.

"They'll *murder* us!" Brenda's whisper, like someone ripping a yard of silk, came from behind. She was referring, of course, to the women at the camp. I kept going, urging her forward, and finally, at a safe distance, stopped, breathless, and said, "I have a better idea. I think we can get in without clipping the fence. Come back to the road."

At the road I began to walk back toward the car. "One of these houses," I said, "is being painted. There's a ladder leaning against the wall."

"Jesus!" But she trotted along.

The house was only a short way down the road, half shiny new color, half faded old color, beige or gray, it was hard to tell. A single light shone behind the blinds in a front room, the rest of the house was dark, and the six-foot ladder stood against a windowless section of a side wall, a closed can of paint at its foot.

"Can you *believe* it?" Brenda, the urbanite, six locks on the door and an iron grille over the windows, was awestruck. "What, nobody breaks *in* around here?"

"Quiet!" I cautioned. "I mean *mute.*"

We moved across the short-cropped lawn, scarcely breathing, lowered the ladder to its side by moving it at a rate of one foot per minute, and, each of us hooking an arm around one end, were about to begin the return trip, when Brenda's foot struck the can of paint.

It wasn't much of a sound, a small thud. To my ear, it reverberated like the opening seconds of a J. Arthur Rank movie. I stood still, trying to invent a plausible excuse for carrying off someone's beat-up stepladder in the dark of night, but no one emerged from the house to investigate. Without looking back to see if Brenda was still conscious, I continued my stealthy progress toward the road and

7

across it to the meadow side, assuming, from the fact that the other end of the ladder was not dragging on the ground, that Brenda was alive and functioning. We had yet to pass two more houses on the other side before the clearing opposite which we'd previously struck across the meadow.

"Somebody's going to come out their front door and see us," Brenda prophesied, "or look out a window and yell, 'Hey, you,' or a car is going to come down the road—"

"Just *walk*."

We reached the section of meadow across from the clearing, and a problem presented itself: how to carry a ladder while crouching. Ultimately we held it like a stretcher between us and hobbled, with agonizing slowness, toward the hickory tree near the fence.

Brenda's tearing whisper announced, "Maggie! I just had a terrible thought!"

I would have said, "I find that hard to believe," but irony loses something when whispered.

"When we land on the ground," she explained, "from a six-foot jump, it'll make noise!"

Well, some, I supposed. Baryshnikovs we weren't. And even he, once or twice, coming down from a five-minute levitation, had evoked a soft grunt from the stage floor. "Earth," I assured her, "is pliant."

Then we were too close to the fence for speech. In silence we struggled on, reached the fence, and in the denser darkness under the hickory boughs, opened the stepladder and set it up sideways against the fence. The ground was uneven: the ladder wobbled. We shifted it a few inches to right and to left and finally settled for relative stability. I signaled that I would hold it steady while she took the first leap. She shook her head vigorously. *She* wasn't going to find herself alone with the military cops. So be it. I mounted to the top of the ladder and stepped out into the air. It was only when I landed—with a muffled thump and a stagger—that it occurred to me I might easily have jumped short and been punctured by barbed wire as it caught a fold of clothing.

Too late to warn Brenda. A pale glimmer of legs left the ladder and I waited for the inevitable "Shit!" but she thumped down beside me and there we were. On the base. Neither of us moved, peering into the dark to see if our arrival had roused anyone. Apparently not. The only sound, after a minute or two, was that of a car rolling sedately over a base road far away. We stood up, cautiously, and I looked back through the barbed wire at our means of escape. We had to get the ladder over the fence but every minute we spent on the base was a risk; all I wanted was to get it over with, we could worry about the ladder when we were leaving. I conveyed the decision to Brenda with one word. "Later."

Looking for landmarks to guide us back, we moved carefully toward the distant light that signaled a facility of some sort. The grass we walked through was still field grass, untended, a sort of buffer zone between the fence and the base proper. Then we reached a base roadway and, beyond it, the neat, clean, manicured contours of an Air Force installation. Somewhere out there in the dark were tennis courts, golf course, ski trails, Olympic-size pool, bowling lanes, theater, duplex apartments, bank, market, service station: a combination Rock Resort and city-state within a superstructure of planes, bombs, radar, research, and alert response routes.

That much I knew from literature I'd read at the camp. What I didn't know then was that somewhere in that well-appointed complex, was a person whose presence on the base that night would result in the kind of havoc that crime generally leaves in its wake.

From where we stood we saw only the distant silhouette of a twin-domed building, almost certainly a hangar, and, closer, a long knife-cut bisecting the shaved grass, which could only mean we'd found what we were looking for. To make certain, we continued until there was no question that what we were looking at was the runway. *The* runway. Planes that rolled down this runway would not be taking off for a package tour of Paris and the château country, not for the Bahamas, not for the Swiss Alps. There would be no Kodak snaps to be printed after these flights, no *Me, buying a djellaba at the market in Tangiers.*

Brenda pointed. The runway ended a hundred yards or so to our right. Fine. This was it, then. It had taken seven minutes to the runway from where we'd entered the base, and there seemed to be no permanent patrol at this end. All that remained was to get back to the camp and report our findings. We turned to leave.

A large man in uniform stood there, watching us, one hand lightly on his holster.

Stood there like a wall. A high wall, a thick wall. Impenetrable, immovable, indestructible. And experienced. This was no youngster.

I waited for unconsciousness to take over, but it's never around when you need it. Brenda, too, was still on her feet. Belligerently so, in fact.

"What's the problem?" she demanded.

He ignored the question. "ID, please," he said, in a quiet, reasonable voice.

I fished in my pocket. Brenda's shorts had no pockets, neither did the poncho: she'd brought nothing with her but pessimism. I handed over my driver's license and he looked at it. His stance was easy, his manner rather casual, not what I'd expect of a military man. And then I realized there was good reason for that: he was not Air Force. The shirt was a darker blue, the pants darker still. He was one of the security guards. I recognized him now. I'd seen him at the main gate the night before.

He held out an upturned palm to Brenda.

"I left it . . ." she began, and changed course, "I don't have it with me."

"No pass?" he said to me.

Simultaneously I shook my head and Brenda said, "We lost it."

"How'd you get in?"

"We came in just the other side of the swimming pool," I said quickly, feeling reasonably certain that anything recreational would be a goodly distance from where we were.

He tilted his head back and looked down at us. Was I imagining it? Was there amusement lurking behind his eyes? "Cut the fence?"

"No," I said, "we crawled through."

This time I definitely saw a twitch at the corner of his mouth. "I'm going to have to take you in," he said. His voice, I thought, was faintly familiar. Fascinating, the psychology of the captive. Endow your captor with cozy human attributes: look, he's friendly, he's almost smiling, he sounds like someone I've met.

Then he pulled something from his pocket and in a matter of seconds we were handcuffed. I looked incredulously at my wrists. Handcuffed! True, they were not the iron shackles of the old prison movies, just some very tough, light-colored plastic, but still! Handcuffed? *Me?*

He marched us back to the base road we'd previously crossed, where a patrol car stood waiting (how had we not heard it coming?), held the door for us to get in, and drove off, through the carefully cultivated grounds, past the dark shapes of trees and the faint sheen of lawns, past a residential street that could have passed for an affluent neighborhood in a small Eastern seaboard town. In a lamplit window a female figure appeared briefly in silhouette. An officer's wife? Was she happy in that house? In this world of male uniforms? Did she walk the dog, laugh with her friends, get her hair done, without any qualms, in the shadow of those planes?

One thing was sure: she sat on a sofa in comfort while I sat in a patrol car in custody. What would Elliot say? Something highly emotional, no doubt: "Will you be out in time to take the car for inspection?" And our two sons, in their postcollege maturity? Embarrassed, most likely. What I'd done was piddling. The women they knew would probably have climbed that chain-link fence, disarmed the

11

man in the beret and crippled the B52s. My mother, of course, would be thrilled but worried about the dampness in prison. And Greenfield? Charles Benjamin Greenfield, ex-broadcast newswriter, father of three ex-chain-link-fence climbers, grand vizier for the last two decades of the *Sloan's Ford Reporter,* he who paid my salary, criticized my syntax, and enriched my life with caustic companionship? "When Zola," he'd say, "incurred the wrath of the military, it was for writing an article that became journalistic history, not for jumping over a fence."

I looked at the security guard. What now? They could hardly put us in a cell just for trespassing. Or could they? Oh God, if only I'd gritted my teeth and gone to that depressing civil disobedience workshop. I didn't even know what to plead.

Brenda, beside me, squirmed and muttered, and the security guard said, "Are you with the peace camp? Or did you come to Hunegger for the tourist attractions?"

A sense of humor? Who would have thought—? I looked at my wrists and came back to reality.

Brenda was in her element now: civilian cops she could handle, the city streets were full of them. "We don't have to answer that," she said.

"Why did you come here?" He addressed the question to me. I looked at him. He looked nothing like Greenfield and yet there was a certain unlikely similarity. Quiet curiosity, I decided. And an absence of fear. His question echoed. *Why did I come here?* How could I answer that truthfully? I winced, remembering.

As motives go, mine was not one of the more glorious in recorded history.

"I came here," I said quite honestly, "because it was spring."

CHAPTER TWO

A WEEK EARLIER I'D BEEN IN GREENFIELD'S office on second floor of the old white house on Poplar Avenue, playing with the word processor his three daughters had given him on his last birthday and which he'd left standing on an old typewriter table, covered and untouched for six months now, repelled by "the vulgarity of the concept that language could be processed, like sausage meat." I was waiting for Greenfield to return from a meeting with Assemblyman Intrado. Normally Greenfield would no more seek out a politician's company than he would a scorpion's, but the state's intention of allowing transport of nuclear waste along a route that ran within a quarter mile of the village center had forced this temporary alliance. He was taking it badly.

Greenfield was a man whose demeanor at the best of

times hardly evoked the lilting strains of *Gaîté Parisienne*. He saw too much, knew too much, and cared too much to have any truck with frivolity: irony was as close as he got. He spoke in a quiet voice that nevertheless could reach the last row in the third balcony, had a wit made of lye, and a fortitude born of a bedrock premise that life was a poorly engineered highway running through collapsing tunnels and flirting with the edges of crumbling cliffs, protected only by cheaply constructed guardrails. In the time I'd known and worked for him we'd shared a hundred meals, several hundred verbal duels, a good deal of music, and four unlooked-for brushes with crime, and I was accustomed to his face.

At the moment, though, what with Intrado and the nuclear waste, life with Greenfield was a little like living on a geographical fault. He was working himself up to a blistering editorial on governmental maladministration, and if the creative tremor brought the walls down on those of us who worked for him, too bad, *sauve qui peut*.

I was not in the most serene of humors myself. Ordinarily I would not be lounging around Greenfield's office in his absence, but I'd come to deliver my two hundred words on the opening of the new village library, and stayed when he left because I didn't know where I wanted to go or what I wanted to do with the remainder of the afternoon. I was edgy, restless, afflicted with an undefined, free-floating yearning.

I looked through the open front window at the froth of new green decorating the trees. It was spring.

Spring, I thought. The burgeoning of all that is free, joyous and feebleminded. On the whole, winter was safer. In winter weather people were reasonably cynical, sensibly depressed, intelligently self-protective and aloof. Temptation was at a low ebb. It was a season for reason. Survival was all.

But spring—! Never mind that the skies are gray and dripping, spring is pre-sold. Centuries of sonnets, couplets, rhymes, have seen to the indoctrination. Browning

14

with his "hillside dew-pearled," Swinburne's "slain frosts and flowers begotten," the Rubaiyat, flinging "the Winter garments of Repentance in the fire of Spring." One new blade of grass, one breath of warm, earth-smelling air, and the flinging begins: coats flung off, windows flung up, emotional gates flung wide. The first gentle breeze, the first dandelion in the lawn, and there's more damage done than by any January blizzard. I turned away from the windows.

The telephone rang.

I should have let it ring. I should have said "No," when that voice asked if it could speak with Mr. Greenfield. I should have said, "Sorry, wrong number." I should, as a last resort, have cut the telephone wire, run out of the office, down the narrow stairway, past the deserted ground-floor rooms from which the latest edition of the *Sloan's Ford Reporter* had just been dispatched, out the front door, around to the back of the house and up the two flights of stairs to Greenfield's living quarters, there to disable his other telephone, dash back, and be found sitting innocently on the crumbling upholstery of one of the old office armchairs by the time Greenfield got back.

Instead, I said, "Who's calling?"

"This is Penelope Heath-Morecomb."

The tone was parliamentary. The accent was British. The implication was that Greenfield would be well advised to get to the phone before the combined misunderstandings at Buckingham Palace, 10 Downing Street and the Foreign Office resulted in a breaking of diplomatic ties between our two countries.

"I'm with the A.C.M.P.," the voice went on.

A.C.M.P. A British branch, no doubt, of the Royal Canadian Mounties.

"And I've been stranded in— Sorry, what's the name of your village?"

"Sloan's Ford."

"Sloan's Ford. I'm driving a hire-car which seems to have collapsed. I'm stuck here for the night, and I badly need rescue."

15

"I think you have the wrong Greenfield."

"Charles Benjamin. Cello. Or so it says in my North American Directory."

Her what?

"This Mr. Greenfield runs a newspaper," I began, and then I heard the front door open and Greenfield's step on the stairs. "Hold on a minute." I put my hand over the mouthpiece.

Greenfield's tread was unhurried, as usual. He was brisk only on the few occasions when he wasn't contemplative, and right now he had plenty to think about. Knowing him, he'd write no editorial until he could offer alternatives to the procedure contemplated by the state, and ten to one Intrado had come up with nothing sensible, he'd have to do it himself. He appeared on the landing and crossed the room like Noah mentally rehearsing what he would suggest to the Almighty as a better way of punishing a wayward people.

I held out the phone. "Someone from British Intelligence," I told him, "needs a garage mechanic who plays the cello."

He took the receiver without so much as a disapproving eyebrow at the whimsical information, dropped his long frame into the swivel chair and leaned back. The chair greeted his familiar weight with its customary asthmatic screech, and he said, "This is Greenfield."

He was dressed for spring: tan corduroys instead of winter brown, beige pullover instead of the pewter. The long, angular face, the mild gaze that fronted for the stinging judgments, the wispy, smoke-colored hair, were the same winter or summer. Listening, he leafed through his notes on the meeting with Intrado.

"Yes," he said into the phone, disclosing nothing.

What was she saying? Who was she? What did she mean by *North American Directory?* I envisioned some gigantic book of records that listed not only three hundred million names, but the occupations, hobbies and political affiliations that went with them. Big Brother . . .

After a number of "I see's," he said, "We have one or two things in fairly good shape, but you notice the B rating?" Then, "Well, you've been warned." And finally, "It's possible. Give me the number on that telephone and I'll see what I can arrange." He found a scrap of virgin paper in a sea of memoranda, tear sheets and clippings, and scribbled. "I'll get back to you as soon as I can." He replaced the receiver, stuck the scribbled phone number on a vertical spike, went back to his notes, searched out another piece of scrap paper, wrote on it and handed it to me.

"This outfit," he said, "has been organized countywide to fight the nuclear-waste decision. Find out who speaks for it and get an interview. Who are they, how big are they, what tactics are they using?"

Not a word about the phone call. He would reveal the nature of Heath-Morecomb's business in his own good time—which, to judge by past experience, could be either tomorrow, or never, or when the snows arrived. Occasionally a show of indifference would speed it up. I pocketed the piece of paper, and, sunk in the lumpy embrace of the second oldest armchair, indicated indifference behind the *Times*.

"The *Times* says they've set up another woman's peace camp, upstate," I volunteered, "at the missile base in Hunegger Mills."

"Hunegger is an Air Force base." He corrected me with the top seventh of his mind, making new notes on his old notes. "Loose terminology in a reporter is on a par with approximation in a brain surgeon."

"They've got missiles there, and until the Air Force flies the missiles out of the base, they're *based* at the *base*. And frankly, I feel a little shabby sitting here writing about new libraries instead of being up there trying to keep the maniacs from incinerating the *old* ones." Until that moment I'd had no idea I was going to say that.

He ignored me.

"I should be up at Hunegger," I repeated, beginning to believe it.

He swiveled slowly around to face me. "No event in the last two thousand years," he said very distinctly, "suggests that the small, scattered voices of intelligence can affect major decisions made in the corridors of power, by men of limited imagination and limitless vanity. The *country* would have to rise. *Twenty* countries would have to rise." He swiveled back to his notes.

"They're not going to rise by themselves. They need a role model."

"Greenham Common hasn't changed anything. Seneca hasn't changed anything. This won't change anything." Thus spoke Zarathustra, on a bad day.

"It's cumulative."

"It's immunization. Familiarity is a vaccine. It prevents exposure to horror from developing into constructive action. The first demonstration may be infectious, the tenth is a soporific. In the meantime we have a nuclear problem in our own backyard, where we might possibly swing enough weight to be effective. Work on it."

"Seems pointless to me, like putting a box of matches out of the baby's reach while the big kids upstairs are setting the mattresses on fire."

No reply. He kept on with his notes. The mood must be even blacker than I'd thought, for Greenfield to abandon an argument without having the last word.

In a few minutes he got up, crossed to the filing cabinet, and asked, sepulchrally, "Do you feel like playing some Mozart tonight?"

"Tonight? This is Wednesday."

He opened the "M" drawer. "I know of no legal injunction, Talmudic proscription, papal Bull or other caveat pertaining to the playing of music on Wednesday." He took a catalogue of some kind from one of the files and turned the pages.

"I thought Gordon was out of town until Friday."

"We don't need Gordon. We have a visiting violinist." He waved a hand at the phone.

A violinist! That British person a violinist? Not one of Smiley's people?

He stopped at a page in the catalogue, read, frowned, marked something on the page and handed it to me.

On the cover I read the words *Amateur Chamber Music Players, Inc.* (Ah! A.C.M.P.) Below that, *International Directory.* The inner pages were covered with lists of names and addresses, four columns to a page, grouped under geographical headings: Australia, Belgium, Denmark, so on. Under *England* Greenfield had circled an entry: *Penelope Heath-Morecomb, VL-PRO, 8 Uxley Close, London, Available weekdays.*

"What's VL-PRO?" I asked.

"The instrument and the rating. She's a professional. A desperate one, apparently, or she wouldn't ask to play with us. Your decision, yes or no?"

I held up the Directory. "Is there a North American version of this?"

"Yes." He removed Heath-Morecomb's phone number from the spike. "Decide, Maggie."

"And you're listed in it and you didn't tell me?"

"Someone sent me a form. I mailed it in and promptly forgot about it. If you feel neglected, you too can be listed, it's simple enough." He lifted the receiver. "The woman is waiting."

I riffled the pages. "This means that if you happen to be in Toledo or Hong Kong or Aberdeen, all you have to do is call someone listed in here and they'll invite you over for a little Mozart? Provided you have your cello with you? Or in my case, my piano?"

Greenfield said nothing. He stood there with the receiver in his hand, eloquently, thunderously silent.

"Fine," I said quickly. "Let's play. Why not?"

I said it. I have no one to blame but myself.

That evening Penelope Heath-Morecomb walked into

my living room trailing the scent of lavender, and proceeded to disrupt several lives.

She had rust-red hair, a sage-green cape, and a compelling presence. Sarah Bernhardt in her prime, were she alive in the 1980s, portraying Queen Elizabeth I in modern dress, would have produced Penelope Heath-Morecomb.

She flashed a brief, public smile, first at Greenfield, then at Elliot, patted George, our red setter, on his head, then stood in the middle of the room, took a deep breath, and said, "That's better. I was suffocating in that cell of a room. For a country that's short on prison space, you're overlooking a good thing in that motel."

Amazingly, I saw a glint of amusement on Greenfield's face.

She clicked her tongue against the roof of her mouth. "Sorry. Not very diplomatic. Travelers are a cruddy lot, aren't they?"

"Are you on tour?" Elliot asked.

"On holiday, actually." She took her violin from its case. "Well, a *working* holiday. But not music work. More important than that at the moment." She ran the bow lightly over the strings, releasing a cascade of silvery notes.

Greenfield, tightening a peg on his cello, looked up sharply. It was a startlingly beautiful sound in that room accustomed to live music of a much more pedestrian, not to say faltering, character.

Nevertheless, it was only a rather beautiful sound. Not the opening of Tutankhamen's tomb. Not the unveiling of Michelangelo's *David*. There was no need for Greenfield to sit there transfixed.

Elliot excused himself and went off to the study, dragging a reluctant George with him. Elliot never sat in the living room when we played music. Out of sight he could listen, if he was so inclined, to the parts that went smoothly, and pick up a book when the going got rough.

Heath-Morecomb sat herself down on one of the dining room chairs I'd provided, pushed the sleeves of her silk shirt up to the elbows and leafed through the music on the stand in front of her. "Ah, the Mozart C major."

"It's a bit simple for you," Greenfield said.

Simple for both of them. The piano did all the work in this one.

"Simple Mozart," she said. "That's like simple caviar. No such thing."

He smiled, as though she'd said something witty. Try saying it without that British accent, I thought, and see what you get. At the piano I struck a very percussive A, and they tuned.

"Our performance," Greenfield said, "is going to call for a high degree of tolerance on your part." He said it awkwardly, inasmuch as humility came as naturally to him as modesty to Picasso, but the point was, he *said* it. What was going on here?

She flicked the apology aside with her bow. "Now look here, Mr. Greenfield—" No one, to my knowledge, had ever said "Now look here" to Greenfield and lived to tell of it, but Greenfield merely looked interested."—firstly, I teach young students, you can't shock me, and secondly you are not entertaining a Heifetz or a Perlman. I am a *journeyman* violinist. Though I did once, by sheer luck, record the Brahms concerto, on a minor label, and I rather prefer my version of the last movement to Perlman's. I don't know what he thought he was doing. An absolutely *sublime* performance of the slow movement, then he suddenly comes all over 'The March of the Wooden Soldiers.' Perhaps it was Giulini's idea."

Greenfield smiled. *Smiled.* Where, suddenly, was his damned stygian gloom?

"I must try to find your recording," he said. "I'd like to hear your version."

Obligingly, she launched into the final segment of the slow movement.

Pure, gorgeous sound. Glowing, melting, fading to a whisper.

All right, so she could play. We'd established that. Fine.

I opened the music on my piano rack with a snap, ready to begin.

But Heath-Morecomb, chin lifted, was giving Greenfield a provocative grin. And he was gazing at her from under his gray bramble of eyebrows with what looked suspiciously like pleasure.

"Shall we," I suggested a trifle tartly, "get started?"

Mozart finally rose into the air, to mingle with the balmy, lilac-scented breeze from the open window and the English lavender from behind the violin. But the playing of music proved to be incidental to the main business of the evening, a mere backdrop for the minuet of glances and challenging smiles and lightly ambiguous remarks that were taking place. They had a lovely time. I could have taped my part and mailed it in for all the notice they took of me.

My fingers plodded heavily along, bar after bar, dragging resentment and apprehension in their wake. Over the past half-dozen years I'd seen a good deal of Greenfield, what with one thing and another. We had shared numberless journeys and discoveries, triumphs and disasters, in harmony and in discord. And in all that time his encounters with other women had been notable for their consistent impersonality on his part.

There'd been many an unattached woman, across a crowded or not so crowded room, office, auditorium, airplane cabin, strip of sand, what have you, of reasonable wit, or charm, or at least of notable physical attributes, who might have been expected to light a spark in any virile widower who had not taken vows. But Greenfield's reactions had ranged from a high of courtesy to a low of glazed boredom. And not, I felt sure, because of a consuming passion for his Madame X, the woman we'd never seen but had known for years existed. *That* relationship spoke more of familiar hearth than of fireworks, more of embers than of blaze. That wasn't what kept him from further adventure. He had simply never found the game worth the candle.

So what Greenfield was this, sitting here of a spring evening so bemused that he missed entrances, ignored key changes and forgot repeats? Where was the legendary jaundiced eye? The sharply objective appraisal? The detachment, the barricade, the Do Not Disturb sign?

I began to feel a tightness in the back of my neck, a clenching of my jaw as I thumped away at the keys, creating a volume of sound Mozart never intended.

At one point Greenfield got up to look at my music. "I thought, from the noise, you'd accidentally included a page from *Tannhäuser.* You might try not using the loud pedal."

"I wasn't using a pedal at all."

I softened to a mere fortissimo, trudging on through the Mozart, and, after it, through the serving of coffee and strawberry tart (I was, after all, only there to cater the affair).

Over coffee the Heath-Morecomb floor show continued in apparently undiminished fascination: "You can't go to a debut concert without hearing the bloody Mendelssohn. They'll be playing it in wine bars next." And, "Medical science would do well to study contemporary music. Philip Glass, for example. I've never heard music of such *riveting* tedium. *There's* your nontoxic anesthetic." And, "After he'd given a brilliant performance of the Tchaikowsky, a friend of his came rushing backstage and said, 'You'll *never* surpass this!' and he said, 'Is that praise, or despair?' "

All of that, of course, delivered *bravura.* I looked in vain for even a hint of glazed boredom in Greenfield's eyes. On the contrary. When it was time to leave, Greenfield insisted on driving her the mile and a half back to the motel (she had walked up earlier, both her car and presumably her broom being unavailable), and they went off down the walk to the driveway, their mingled voices receding in the soft spring night.

I shut the door on them. Elliot asked if he could help with the coffee cups. I said no thanks, I could smash them

23

all by myself, surprising both of us with my uncharacteristic behavior. But one thing that has always pushed me askew is being made to feel *superfluous*. And on top of that it was spring.

Later, as I lay awake in the dark, I envisioned Greenfield's Plymouth dawdling down Poplar Avenue in the direction of the village. Slowing to a crawl as it neared the old three-storied, white-sided, mansard-roofed house. Pulling into Greenfield's driveway. Greenfield escorting her up the two flights of stairs to his living quarters to display his humidity-controlled cello cabinet. Offering her a brandy . . .

Yes, it would happen that way. Because I knew now. I knew without having to resort to any genealogical research that Heath-Morecomb's female ancestors had not sprung from British soil. They had arrived there, centuries ago, by swimming up from the Aegean, where they had spent their lives sitting in their meadow by the dangerous rocks, singing seductively and luring unsuspecting sailors like Odysseus to their doom.

Penelope, my foot. Daughter of Achelous was more like it. Sending her bloody spellbinding music out across the waves.

And there went Greenfield, heading for the rocks.

The next day she was gone. "Hired" another car, or got the first one fixed. I had a bright note, thanking me for furthering international goodwill. Goodwill. If ever a thank-you was undeserved.

Greenfield said nothing about her. That spoke for itself. An innocent man would have made at least some passing reference to what was not, after all, a commonplace occurrence in our musical life. Some comment on her performance, her anecdotes, her violin. He might have shared whatever information she'd disclosed after leaving my house, about her background, her marital status, her proposed destination in this primitive colony of the British Empire, how soon, please God, she was planning to return home.

Not a word. Just sat at his desk with a blue pencil in his hand and Stewart's overblown report of a landlord's run-in with the State Division of Housing before him, staring out the window at the bird feeder that swung between the eaves of the house and the branches of the huge maple beyond. There wasn't even a bird on the bird feeder, and he sat gazing at it.

I found myself incapable of mentioning the subject. There were very few subjects I was incapable of mentioning to Greenfield, but this time I was mute. I sensed that this man was not Greenfield but some peculiar impostor. As the week wore on, the conviction grew.

I brought in the results of my meeting with the spokeswoman for the group fighting the nuclear-waste-transport decision—his cause célèbre. Instead of finding three questionable assertions, two instances of superfluous verbiage and a misplaced paragraph, he gave it a glance, handed it back, and said gently, "Why don't you start wearing skirts, Maggie? It's spring."

He walked into the layout room to find that Calli Dohanis had placed a shot of the library staff standing outside the new library over a caption for a picture of wildlife volunteers who'd been trained to take care of injured wild animals. Instead of suggesting that Calli was indebted to him to the tune of six years' salary for the privilege of learning her trade, he said breezily, "Quite a comment, Dohanis. You're becoming another Mencken."

Helen Deutsch came toiling up the stairs to report that the Varityper dial was jammed again, preventing her from achieving any size type but tiny. Instead of rising slowly from his chair like a man whose undeserved afflictions put Job in the shade, he told her blithely not to worry about it, ed cummings had done very nicely in lower case.

He had a message that Intrado had called, and instead of returning the call he disappeared for an entire afternoon and reappeared with packages, one of which, bearing the name of a record store in lower Manhattan forty miles away, he immediately opened, placing the contents on the

25

turntable of his office stereo, where it remained for days, playing the same piece of music, hour after hour. To listen to Brahms is one of the reasons I live, but I wanted never, never again, to hear that violin concerto.

In the downstairs offices the uneasiness was palpable.

"What's the matter with him?" Helen asked.

"Spring."

"I mean *really.*"

"So do I."

"What's the matter with him?" Calli asked.

"Rocks," I said.

Calli nodded sagely and tapped her head. "I always thought so."

"What's the matter with you?" Elliot asked me as I slammed around the kitchen.

"Me?" I said, "there's nothing the matter with me." And shouted, "George! Stop that!" at my dog.

Shouted. At this animal whose well-being I would protect if necessary by fighting a slavering wolf barehanded. Who looked up at me with beautiful, startled eyes, sank slowly to the ground, and put his head quietly down on his paws.

"Maggie. Calm down," Elliot said.

"Elliot, *don't start.*"

He walked out of the room.

By the end of the week the havoc wreaked had reached sizable proportions: I had torn a dishtowel in half because it persisted in falling off its hook, broken a key on my typewriter by yanking it viciously when it stuck, scraped a fender passing a Buick in front of me because the idiot was crawling along at the designated speed limit, and finally alienated Elliot's brother who had called on the phone to say a friendly hello.

"What did he say, that you attacked him like that?" Elliot demanded, after trying to mend the family fences.

"Oh, he was carrying on about some stupid British television series. 'The Brits are the only ones who can carry it off.' I'm bloody sick and tired of the bloody Brits!"

"Then stop using bloody British slang."

"They have a monopoly on that too, do they!"

He gave me what, for Elliot, was a distinctly frosty look. Elliot is a man of incredibly equable temperament, given to an unruffled acceptance of the imperfections of life, but there had been one or two occasions, in the course of twenty-six years, when he had allowed my more febrile nature to provoke him into a real bang-up fight, and this promised to be one more. There was a dangerous light in his eye.

"You'd better climb down off the ceiling," he said, "or there's going to be trouble."

"Going to be! There *is!* There *has* been! There's been nothing *but!* Charlie's lost his mind! I mean *lost* it! The paper's a mess! Nobody can get a decision out of him! Yesterday I tripped over a wire in his office and yanked the plug out and he said, 'Congratulations, you just lost an entire editorial.' He's using the *word processor! Charlie!* And he's bought three new shirts and a *ridiculous* jacket! Where's his dignity? Where's his sense of proportion? He's going to be sixty years old, for God's sake!"

"Cut it out, Maggie."

"Cut *what* out?"

"The jealous tantrums."

I gasped from the blow. I felt the blood leaving my face. I felt it rushing back. I felt my dinner coming up. I raced upstairs.

It was then that I decided to go to Hunegger Mills.

CHAPTER THREE

I TRIED TO TELL MYSELF THIS WAS A PLANNED, rational and obligatory trip I was making to the peace camp, that it sprang from conscience and moral fervor. Driving north on the Thruway, I tried to breathe slowly, deeply and regularly, tried to keep my speed down to a mere sixty-five, tried to look with interest at the scenic wonders that passed my windows: gas stations, truck farms, Wright's Plumbing Supplies. It was only after the State Police car cut in front of me and the large uniform waved me to the side of the road, handed me a ticket and informed me that the Indianapolis speedway was in the other direction, that I wiped my wet palms on my jeans, pulled carefully out again into traffic, and admitted that this was, plainly and simply, a frantic escape.

To avoid seeing both Greenfield and Elliot for a while

I would have driven to Butte, Montana. Rouen, Quebec. Fairbanks. Anywhere, to turn my back on that welter of incoherent emotions.

Jealous tantrums. What idiocy! Couldn't he tell anger from jealousy? I was furious, by God, because Greenfield was behaving like an irresponsible idiot. Jealous! If anyone was jealous, it was Elliot. Jealous because of my alleged jealousy. Which was a manifestly baseless accusation. Had I ever been jealous of Madame X? There you are. Just let Greenfield keep his infatuation to himself and not make the paper suffer for it. What he did on his own time . . . anyway, in the office he was *my* concern. And I was supposed to be his. The office was no place for infatuation. And there was no doubt Greenfield was infatuated. Was there? Was I imagining the whole thing? Did *Elliot* think Greenfield was infatuated? Or had Elliot been so mesmerized he'd failed to notice? Ha! Was Elliot jealous of *Greenfield?* Because Elliot *also* coveted that Brit? Had he accused me because *he* was guilty? Good God, had I lost *both* of them? Had I been run over by mid-life male adolescence? Oh fine, then. Fine. Let them both go. Let her pack them both up in her sage-green cape and carry them back to Uxley Close. She could tuck them up in her "flat" and Brahms them into a stupor. At least I'd no longer have to be the only sober one in a party of drunks.

I needed air. I needed to breathe deeply, to act, do something simple, direct, useful. Preferably where there were no men to worry about. No men to appease, to impress, to satisfy, to contend with, to compete for, to rely on, to be betrayed by, to entertain, seduce, love, loathe, *care* about.

I drove on. It was a long drive. Time enough for the fever to cool, for realistic appraisal to creep in around the edges of impulse. A peace camp. Full of nineteen-year-olds. I would melt into the crowd like Jane Austen at a disco. A peace camp, full of passive resisters who thought nothing of lying down in the dust in the path of military vehicles, being hauled by the armpits over dirty roads, herded into smelly cells in police stations. I would be the only clean one. A peace camp, full of believers, young women of total conviction, unquestioning commitment, burning faith. I would be the only agnostic.

It was entirely possible I was too far along the span of life, too fond of my habits, too eclectic in my thinking, to be any good at this. I naturally defended my position when Greenfield attacked, but left to myself I was far from certain we could make enough of an impact to change anything at all.

Nevertheless.

Adrift in a lifeboat a thousand miles from any hope of ship or plane, one nevertheless sent up flares. Terminally isolated on an icy mountain peak, one kept moving or died. Faced with missiles, one marched.

I drove on.

It was late afternoon when I reached Hunegger Mills' main street, a short stretch of somewhat seedy one- and two-story buildings: Stan's Garage, the Mills Café, a laundromat with a plastic curtain over the bottom half of the window. It was very quiet, no one about but one pale young woman wheeling a baby in a stroller. I parked behind a badly rusted car belonging to the Fire Department, in front of a hardware store where a small American flag stood at attention among the rakes, watering cans and Quick Turf in the window, went into the store and asked the way to the peace camp.

The man behind the counter had a ruddy complexion, a flattened nose, and all the time in the world. He came outside with me and reeled off a list of street names and route numbers while pointing north, east, south, west, and east again. I thanked him, got back in the car and followed what I could remember of the directions.

The route took me into the adjacent town of Padua, a small municipality that somehow achieved the proportions of a metropolis when juxtaposed to the scrap of a village that was Hunegger Mills. Somewhere between Hunegger and Padua was the Air Force base, and not far from the base was the camp. Driving north, east, and north again, I was beginning to feel sure I'd taken a wrong turn somewhere and was heading for the Canadian border, when I found myself passing the main entrance to Hunegger Air Force Base.

I pulled in at the curb opposite the entrance, and stared at the scene before me. Two or three dozen women had gathered in front of the gate, some sitting cross-legged on the ground, some leaning against the fence, some shaking it, some tying themselves to it.

And they were chanting:

"Nuclear bombs are boomerangs!"

"This is the only earth we have!"

"Arms for hugging, not arms for killing!"

On my side of the road a group of townspeople stood watching the show; men in jeans and in business suits, women in slacks and in print dresses, teenagers wearing T-shirts and shorts and self-conscious smirks. One woman crossed the road with a plate of cookies to offer to the protesters. Another one called out, "Go on home, leave us alone!" A man with shirt sleeves rolled above bulging biceps shouted, "Commies!" An old woman with a single roller in her hair asked a younger woman, "What are they doing, Irmie?"

A deputy from the county sheriff's department leaned against his patrol car nearby, ready for trouble.

I thought: Is this it? Is this the massive demonstration I traveled all day to join?

I'd somehow had in mind a picture of the French Revolution: an unmilitary army of aroused citizens storming the barricades, a sea of crusading humanity, wave upon wave of the peace-loving and life-revering, crashing against the gates of unholy destruction. This looked like very small potatoes.

And it certainly wasn't the campgrounds. I crossed the road to ask one of the women for further directions. At the fence a small, delicate girl with Oriental features was poking a pamphlet through the chain link trying to get the security guard on the other side to take it. He was a big, thick, six-foot-four, arms like tree trunks, eyes like granite, keeping his expression noncommittal as he looked down at her serious little face. Gargantua and Yum-Yum. Turning away from the fence, she saw me and proffered one of the pamphlets.

"I'm looking for the peace camp," I told her.

"Yes!" she chirped, and pointed, "Is there. One mile and half."

It was. Exactly one and a half miles.

A sign by the side of the road, a banner stretched between two six-foot metal stakes driven solidly into the ground by some arm of the weaker sex, said WOMEN'S CAMP FOR PEACE. Close by the road, at a stand marked *Information,* two girls behind a plank of counter were gathering up piles of leaflets, preparing to close down for the day. Beyond them, in a meadow of unkempt, trampled grass, stood an assortment of parked vehicles, and in the middle distance, linked to the road by a dirt track, a large weathered gray barn on a stone foundation, all that was left, apparently, of a once working farm. A charred, uninhabited farmhouse stood at some distance from the barn, blackened window frames and drunken front door hanging askew, testifying to some crippling disaster.

I stopped at the Information stand, was directed to the barn and told to see "JoAnne or Harriet," bounced up the track, and parked beside a dusty station wagon. There were women everywhere, walking in and out of the barn, crossing the field beyond it, standing in animated discussion in groups of four or five, swatting at flies and shifting around uncomfortably sitting in a circle on the rough ground listening to a lean-faced woman in overalls. A weary-looking group in the distance seemed to be erecting some kind of shelter, struggling with two-by-fours, wielding hammers. I was relieved to see they all seemed to be over nineteen. None of them, however, had made it to the watershed mark.

A door in a sort of lean-to attached to the side of the

barn opened into a small, low-ceilinged room, where a stocky young woman wearing thick blue-rimmed glasses and the expression of a contentious university student was speaking into a telephone, her backside propped against an old kitchen table laden with cartons of pamphlets and leaflets and several coffee-stained mugs.

"A slash. Right down the wall of the tent. With a knife. And her watch was missing. Now, nobody in this camp is going to do something like that. No, there have *not* been any arguments. This is clearly harassment from the town. Vandalism. Destruction of personal property. Now, Sheriff Slater is supposed to be responsible for protecting . . . Well, let me talk to him. . . . Well, when is he going to be back? . . . Well, what's going to be done about this?" She saw me and raised a pair of ruler-straight eyebrows.

"Harriet?" I said.

She gestured to a door on her left and said into the phone, "I know what you *can't* do, what *are* you going to do?"

I opened the door leading into the barn proper. Motes of dust danced in the late-afternoon light that came from windows high up near the rafters. The rough wood planking of the floor stretched unbroken down the middle of the barn to the far end where a ladder rose to what I assumed had been a hay loft, but on either side crude plywood walls had been put up, sectioning the interior into room-size stalls. There was a smell of damp wood and machine oil and ink, and a buzz of overlapping voices.

From beyond the first partition a voice said, "Well, I just don't think that's enough meat for the whole staff."

A second voice observed, "Better a short ration at a friendly board than a hamburger at the Mills Café."

In a cubicle on the opposite side a meeting of some kind seemed to be in progress. A dozen heads, fair, dark and in-between, bent over some papers on a table.

"Well look, does it belong in Community Relations or in Media? Seems to me—"

Three girls with bedrolls under their arms appeared from the back of the barn.

"I'm looking for JoAnne or Harriet," I said to them.

"Harriet!" one of them called.

A short woman with tousled gray hair came out from behind a partition, exuding amiable calm. "Problem?" she inquired. A soft, domestic-looking woman, durable as steel and well beyond the watershed.

"Somebody to see you."

Harriet gave me a small smile, put a hand lightly on my arm to detain me while she asked the others, "Why the sleeping bags?"

"We're going to spend the night at the gate."

"Remember, no physical or verbal violence. Don't tangle with the people from town."

One of the girls laughed. "There's one I wouldn't mind tangling with."

Harriet gave her a sweet, steely look.

"Not to worry, Harriet," said another. "Duty before lust."

Harriet led me into the "office": a secondhand desk covered in correspondence, a weathered table holding a thirty-year-old Remington portable, a rack of hotel-style mail slots on the wall, one bench and three old kitchen chairs. I told her I wanted to join the camp. She told me I should have registered in advance.

I said I hadn't realized it was necessary. Well, not vital, she said, but that was the procedure; however, it was more important in the case of a group, a single individual could, at the moment, be accommodated. She gave me a mimeographed form to fill out. Name, address, PLEASE LIST ANY SKILLS THAT MIGHT BE USEFUL TO THE CAMP.

Skills? I couldn't see a peace camp needing a pianist, and I was damned if I was going to make beds, mow lawns, sit at a typewriter or cook *daube niçoise*. "I work for a small-town newspaper," I told her, "but I didn't come here to do that."

She stood looking at me, the form, with my vital statistics, now in her hand. "A reporter," she murmured unhappily.

We talked for a few minutes about my convictions and my ostensible reasons for joining the camp, while her mind was busy assessing me. She couldn't very well find some pretext to turn me down, the camp wouldn't risk making an enemy of even a lowly member of the press. On the other hand, she was certainly going to keep an eye on me. Finally she asked what I'd brought with me in the way of shelter, provisions, clothing and money.

"Campers are required, as a minimum, to be self-sufficient," she said. "The Women's Camp fund is barely enough to provide food for the staff. You can use the facilities in the kitchen shack when available, and you can buy soup and crackers there. Coffee is always available. There's no fee for camping, but contributions are more than welcome." She consulted a diagram of the camping site with names penciled in. "It's just as well you won't need the use of a community tent, we're filling up there." She handed me a sheet of paper. "That's a list of the work divisions, you'll have to join one of them."

I looked at the list and felt my resolve weakening. *Maintenance? Health care? Finance?*

"With your background," she went on, printing my name in tiny letters on the diagram, "you could be very helpful in the Media division."

I pointed out that my knowledge of the camp's background, workings and official goals was less than negligible.

"It wouldn't take you long to learn that."

"I'd rather join something else." I looked down the list of unappetizing prospects. *Food. Orientation. Civil Disobedience.* Thirty years as an adult, and here I was back in my miserable teens. *Well, what's it going to be, Maggie, school orchestra or school paper?* "How about Security?" What could that involve, after all? Taking my turn walking around with a flashlight.

35

"Fine, Doris is in charge of that. You may have seen her in the front office as you came in."

Stocky. Aggressive. Blue-rimmed glasses. My luck was running true to form.

"Of course, everybody signs up for additional work in other areas as needed."

Of course.

A woman came in, holding a sheaf of papers. A peace activist's life seemed to be submerged in paper. "Looks like we've had it with that well," she said. "Otis says it's good and dry. Lantz quoted a price for trucking in water —God, you could buy an ocean for that kind of money, maybe we ought to try what'shisname in West Crannock. I know it's farther—" She noticed me. "A new recruit?"

Harriet said, "Maggie—JoAnne."

JoAnne. A well-boned face, open, forthright, capable and sharply intelligent. Simple, friendly manner, and eyes that would remember the tiny mole under your left ear. Tall, generously endowed body in faded denim skirt, loose shirt, sneakers. About twenty years or more younger than Harriet, which made her a peer.

"You're here alone?" she asked. "Are you going to need some help setting up?"

"Probably. I brought a small camping tent one of my sons left behind when he moved. I've never used it and I suspect I'm not a natural camper."

"Like me. Intestinal fortitude and ten thumbs. Well, let's see who's around."

As she started out, Doris came stomping in, pushing up the bridge of her blue-rimmed glasses with one finger.

"Trouble!" she announced, and took a stance, looking from Harriet to JoAnne and back. "*Alice Dakin . . .* is here."

Harriet went very still. The freckles on JoAnne's face suddenly stood out darkly against her pale skin.

"Here?" she said, poking a thumb toward the floor.

"In Padua."

JoAnne looked at Harriet. Harriet sighed deeply and sat down at the desk.

Alice Dakin. I knew the name, of course. A crusader, out to save the country from a long list of undesirables that included peace activists, feminists, intellectuals, union members, homosexuals, students from the more advanced universities, supporters of Medicare, civil rights and school lunches, aliens, environmentalists, all those in favor of banning handguns, and anyone suspected of being an unregenerate Democrat. With the Bible in one hand, a hair dryer in the other, and her eye firmly fixed on national prominence, Alice Dakin rode fearlessly at the head of a small but loyal army, a sort of Joan of Arc of prejudice.

"Where did you hear this?" JoAnne asked.

"Some of the girls saw her. She stopped at the main gate."

"Maybe she's just passing through," Harriet said, without hope.

Doris scoffed, "On her way to what, a cow pasture?"

"We'll have to find out." Harriet fiddled with a pen on the desk. "Is there anyone around who can give Maggie a hand with her tent?"

The hand they found belonged to a girl called Lotte. Sturdy, unflinching, full of common sense and bootstrap principles. West German. In the field beyond the barn it took her no more than ten minutes to set up the tent, and would have taken five without my help.

"That's very good," she decided. "Try it."

I looked down at my abode. Knee-high and cone-shaped, it looked like a large, grounded wind sock. An oversized, opaque butterfly net. I unrolled the foam sleeping mat, parted the fly and slipped the mat in on the coated nylon floor.

"Go in," Lotte urged. "It's not going to hurt you."

I crawled in and lay down flat on my back. It was a nylon space capsule. A high-tech doghouse. It was hospital equipment: eventually they would pull out my head

37

and take a CAT Scan. All I could see of the outside world was a small triangle of grass and sky through the net of the fly: if not for that, claustrophobia would instantly grip me. I crawled out.

"Lovely," I said, clearing my throat. "Thank you. It's fine."

"You see—" Lotte undid a small roll at the top of the opening and a flap came down over the fly, virtually sealing the capsule. "That's for when the rain comes."

Rain. An open meadow, spread out under the sky, stretching back from the barn to the dark, wooded horizon. Not a tree closer than the woods a quarter of a mile away. No spreading chestnut, no overhanging boughs of elm or ash. A direct line from storm clouds to tents. Sitting ducks.

Lotte saw my apprehensive glance at the sky. "Oh *come,*" she said, "*come.* You're afraid for a little water?"

We started back over the meadow toward the barn, threading our way through the tents; the old A-frames, the new Sierra models, the tents improvised from sheets of heavy plastic draped over wooden poles, a collection of shapes that suggested everything from igloos to tepees.

"There's bigger things to be afraid for," Lotte informed me, "as water from the sky. Be glad if you have only that worry."

She was obviously a courageous, dedicated young woman. She'd traveled a long way to fight for her principles. She'd agreed to help me put up the tent without a moment's hesitation, and done the job cheerfully and expertly. But smug is smug.

"I love rain," I lied. "I walk for miles in the rain."

"Good. Maybe we have to, on Saturday."

"Why Saturday?"

"The march! The big march! Hundreds of people coming! Might be thousands! From here, to Hunegger, to Padua, to the base. A long march." She looked down at my sandals. "You need better shoes. If you march."

"Of course I'll march!" If I survive the tent, and the

rain, and the long trailer-like building that I'd been told housed the portable toilets.

In front of the barn, standing by a battered red van, JoAnne was being harangued by a young man with a brown moustache and sunglasses.

"It's against the law, you know?" he was saying tensely. "It's discrimination. It's a violation of my civil rights."

"I'm sorry." JoAnne was being patient. "We can *not—have—men* living at the camp. It's a *women's* camp. *Deliberately*. Now, don't give me a hard time, we're having public relations problems as it is—"

"All I want to do is shoot some atmosphere, tape some attitudes, you can *edit* the stuff if you want—"

"You can *imagine* what they'd be saying if we had *men* staying in the—"

A second young man stepped out of the van. "Mike, why don't we just . . ."

"There is no way you can camp here."

"A videotaped documentary of the protest—you can't *buy* that kind of exposure."

"Videotape, fine. Camping, no. *No*." I'd heard people take a firm stand before, but JoAnne's would still be standing when all the others had collapsed. I made a mental note never to waste time arguing with her.

I went to my car and collected my bag, wondering whether there would be room at the foot of the tent for both it and my two legs, and whether the cause of freedom from annihilation would truly be served by my handing myself over to the animal life that would undoubtedly crawl in during the night. A perceptible coolness was creeping into the air as I headed back to the tent. A young woman in red shorts came walking toward me and stopped as we drew level.

"Hi." She held out a hand. "Brenda."

I gave her my hand and my name.

"You just get here?" She had short, dark curls and the bright, wary, street-smart face of the city-bred.

"More or less. I was just thinking about finding something to eat. Is there a decent restaurant somewhere nearby?"

"You going into town? Okay if I go with you?"

She didn't own a car, she'd come up on the bus. The night before, she'd shared a tent-cooked meal with her tentmates. "From Elks Corners and Canada and Akron, Ohio, and like that. They've got a two-burner propane stove. Everything's dehydrated or freeze-dried. Dehydrated cheese omelet—you ever taste squashy plasterboard? Dehydrated hash-browns. Freeze-dried yogurt. I don't know how they're not all in the hospital. Even the Mills Café is better."

I remembered the Mills Café from my short stop in Hunegger: a luncheonette of clapboard siding with decals of flowers pressed on the windows and PIZZA hand-lettered on a piece of cardboard, in crayon.

"Is there something better than the Mills Café?"

"Look, this is upstate. If you're expecting tabouleh or sushi, forget it. We could go to the Sycamore, I guess, but that means I have to put on some pants."

She went back to her community tent while I put my bag in the wind sock. She reappeared wearing magenta cotton trousers designed by some contemporary genius who had clearly been inspired by early George Raft movies. We drove away from the camp, Brenda directing me through the back roads, past a cornfield and a beanfield, past a stretch of prim, isolated frame houses, each standing on its own island of tidy lawn and separated from its distant neighbor by a few acres of wild vegetation. We crossed a small iron bridge that spanned a meandering stream, circled a monument marking the site of some Revolutionary War battle, wheeled down the main street of Hunegger Mills to the village outskirts and onto the road leading to the sizable town of Padua, and finally ascended to the brow of a short hill, where the Sycamore Inn, with a Greek Revival façade attached to its standard motel entrance, stood in a mini-estate of lawns, flower beds and "guest cottages."

In the lobby a noticeboard standing on an easel announced to those interested that the thirtieth reunion of the Padua Community College class of '54 was even now taking place in the dining room. Brenda threw up her hands and turned to leave, but I walked up to the dining room entrance.

Fifty or sixty classmates sat around a clutch of tables that sported floral centerpieces and conspicuous bottles of champagne, packing away roast chicken and broccoli, sipping at their glasses, chattering, giggling, guffawing, with that combination of strain and self-conscious merriment such occasions engender. But there were a number of flowerless, champagneless tables and at least three of them were occupied by unaffiliated diners.

I motioned to Brenda and we walked into the room. At our entrance there was a chain reaction of suspended motion among the classmates of '54. It lasted no longer than a sneeze, but it was just as unmistakable: the old frontier saloon. Through the swing doors The Strangers enter, and all down the long, brass-railed bar, the grizzled, hard-drinking men fall silent.

By the time we reached a table, conversations had been resumed, cutlery clattered again, glasses were raised and lowered. I sent a questioning glance across the table to Brenda. "This town ain't big enough for the two of us?"

"They can tell we're from the camp."

"How?"

She shrugged. I looked across at the revelers, ranks closed against a common threat. "I suppose the camp seems like an invasion."

"They think we want to close down the base, take away their jobs and ruin their economy."

A waitress arrived, all seventeen bread-pudding years of her. She smiled tightly, treading a careful line between professional courtesy and consorting with the enemy, and we ordered. My watch said five past seven. Elliot would be sitting at our dining room table with a lonely lamb chop.

"I think I'll make a quick call while we're waiting." So much for escape. I left Brenda hungrily buttering a roll, found a public telephone in the lobby, dialed the collect call, heard the busy signal. While I stood there waiting for the line to be free, the door marked LADIES opened and two women emerged, one in lacy knit two-piece with pearls, the other in a pastel suit that would never wrinkle any more than sheet metal would. They hovered in age between forty-nine and resignation. Class of '54 if ever there was one.

Knit-and-pearls searched feverishly in her white summer bag. "Did I leave my pillbox in the—? I swear, this thing has me so upset—"

The pastel suit, a woman with the officious look of a civil servant at a motor vehicle bureau, was dabbing her forehead with a tissue. "How does Lynette feel about it?"

"Oh, Lynette." The pearls hung forward as she searched in the bag. A memory of prettiness hung like a film over slightly pendulous cheeks and shrinking blue-shadowed eyes. "Lynette's in another world. You know. It's Bruce, Bruce, morning, noon and night. I don't think she'd notice if we had the wedding in the middle of the highway, at quitting time. And we might as well. Can you imagine coming out of the church into that—!"

"I hear they're expecting five thousand demonstrators. The base is bringing in extra military police."

"They're *what?* Frank didn't tell me that."

"Two hundred extra police, I heard."

"I'm going to have a nervous breakdown, Ethel. How are we going to get from the church to the reception? The streets will be— There'll be violence, I know it. Why did they have to pick this weekend!" She ran a nervous hand over her thick dark hair.

"Bunch of terrorist screwballs. What they're doing to this town is a crime. I told you we had this man ready to close the deal on buying the store? Well, there's been a delay. Delay my foot. Had second thoughts, more like it. Who wants to take over a business in a town that runs into this kind of trouble? Connie, you're going to tear a hole in that bag. Look in the Ladies', maybe you—"

I tried the number again. Still busy. The two women reemerged from "the ladies'," the civil servant still talking.

"And Patty Semak is having a fit. They were supposed to go on vacation, then suddenly Mac comes home and says Slater told them, 'We've got this big protest on our hands and all deputy leaves are hereby canceled.' Patty had made reservations at the lake, the kids were all set to go, now they're sulking. . . ."

They went off to the dining room.

I got through. Elliot had been on the phone with Alan, the elder son, whose reaction to the news of my whereabouts had been one of mild incredulity: he was preoccupied with his own two incessant problems, job and girl. I told Elliot I was fine, and yes, I was staying for a while. He told me he might have to go out of town for a few days and would let me know. I gave him the number of the telephone at the camp. We exchanged a few more civilized remarks and I replaced the receiver. Had he seemed a little less withdrawn? A fraction less?

He hadn't said much when I'd made my announcement —merely, "I thought, when the boys outgrew it, I was through with summer camp." And turned over and pretended to go to sleep.

I rejoined Brenda, we ate chicken and drank coffee to the accompaniment of the class of '54's merrymaking. Brenda, one-quarter partner in a six-table Tribeca eatery called Sammy Chun's Bagels, found the food "Typical dull. You mention ethnic around here they think it's a virus." We paid the check, left the Sycamore, and drove off to put in our stint at the main gate of the base.

The darkening countryside smelled sweet and clean— hay, dew-drenched grass, and from somewhere a whiff of mock orange blossoms. It seemed impossible that what was sitting behind that Air Force fence a few miles away was really there.

I told Brenda about the conversation I'd overheard in the lobby.

"Oh sure," she said, "we're screwballs. We're troublemakers. *They're* sitting here, a couple of miles from missiles that could blow everybody in this whole state into *confetti*—if they're *lucky*—and *we're* the crazy ones."

I remembered Greenfield's "The *country* would have to rise. *Twenty* countries would have to rise."

These people rise? Where would they find the time? They had daughters to marry off, businesses to sell, vacations they'd been waiting to take. They had wages to earn, children to clothe and feed and school and nurse through fevers, cars that broke down, aged mothers and fathers who couldn't be left alone, shirts to iron, meals to prepare, reunions to attend. It all took *time,* this business of living. It took every minute of the day and half the night. This was the "country" that would have to rise. These working, striving, bill-paying, baseball-watching, movie-going, insurance-buying, bank-depositing, hopeful, worried, busy people. Thanksgiving, Memorial Day parade, Lodge Barbecue. Out of Norman Rockwell and Seventy-Six Trombones to Cable TV, male strippers and computer courses. Where, in all of that, could nuclear war be a reality?

The main entrance to the base was flooded with harsh white light. The women were there—more, it seemed, than there had been earlier—in their jeans and T-shirts and overalls and whatnot, shouting questions at the guards, threading colored yarn through the fence-links, kneeling on the driveway with cans of paint and brushes, lettering slogans on the asphalt. There were a few civilians around as well; one of them, pointing his camera at the fence, was the man who'd been haranguing JoAnne at the camp. And one group of women, sitting on the ground, was singing, of all things, "Greensleeves."

All this I took in within seconds, and it was all irrelevant. The image that leaped to my eye, and stayed there, was that of an armed security guard standing behind the fence, eyes riveted, very still, very quiet, very, very watchful. He was not the Gargantua I'd seen earlier, but he was big. And I didn't have to follow his gaze to see what was holding him rapt: the sound told me.

The sound of a violin. A violin, for God's sake! To *charm* the nukes off the planes?

And there she stood, playing along with the singers. She was facing the fence, legs astride, bare British arm flourishing the violin bow, rust-red hair like a dark flame in the white light that separated the outside world from the stern secrets of the Strategic Air Command.

I'd run in a circle.

CHAPTER FOUR

I LAY AWAKE IN THE DARK, HUMID NIGHT, IN MY papoose-carrier of a tent, tensely remembering that some-one's knife had earlier ripped through some nearby nylon wall. (And it would be my job, from now on, to confront whoever tried it next!) I was exhausted from the long day, too full of impressions and reactions to sleep.

Crickets inhabited the night, keeping up an endless chirp. Small things stirred in the grass around the tent. A car swooshed by far down on the road. Closer, there was a hollow clank: someone's canteen knocking against a tent pole?

Behind my determinedly closed eyelids, persistent images chased each other in maddening succession; JoAnne saying "No!" to the man with the camera, Brenda's magenta pants, the battle monument in Hunegger Mills, Connie of the knit-and-pearls searching in her bag, the stocky girl's glasses glinting as she enunciated *"Dakin—is—here,"* the security guard watching behind the fence, Heath-Morecomb's look of approval at sight of me.

Approval. Who was she to approve or disapprove of me!

"Maggie Rome," she'd said, seeing me. Not an exclamation, not surprise, but an assessment. "Brava!"

I'd considered going back to the camp, packing up and leaving, late as it was.

Around us the women chanted and raised their arms, wrists crossed in the international peace sign.

"Last place I expected to see you," I'd managed to say, in a neutral tone.

"Why, I'm a veteran," she'd answered with a suggestion of dry amusement, "six months at Greenham Common. You have it posh here, by comparison. You should have seen us over there, all mucky boots and holes in the ground for toilets. What was it like at Seneca?"

"I wasn't there."

"I would have been, but I was short of the fare at the time. No loot. *Pas d'argent.* Now I'll miss it again. I can't stay on here forever." She transferred the bow to the hand holding the violin and wiped the free hand on her jeans. I caught the scent of lavender.

I gestured at the violin. "Is that what you did at Greenham?"

She gave me a sharp look. "A bit more than that. Don't underestimate this, though." She swung the violin gently. "Makes strong men weep, used properly."

Does it, though.

"It says: *This is peace. This is life. This is what you're going to destroy.*"

"And *they* say, 'Go play it in Moscow.' And they have a point."

She looked down at the violin and said, in a breezy manner that nevertheless conveyed an indestructible will, "I shall play this violin in Moscow one day. And I shall play it in the Middle East and in Asia and in the

47

Antipodes and wherever it needs to be played, until those unspeakable horrors"—without looking up she flung an arm toward the fence—"have been buried, in imperishable steel, below the nethermost layer of minerals in the soil of this earth." She swept up a hat from where it had fallen on the ground, and plunked it on her titian hair. Applause. Curtain. The hat was a straw boater, with a wide white band around it bearing in black letters the word BAND, a bit of kitsch that surprised me, considering her sophistication.

Over her shoulder I saw the security policeman still watching her. I didn't blame him, she looked like trouble. She looked volatile, febrile, incendiary. I made an excuse to turn away, reading the slogans the women had painted, and she went back to her singers.

I saw it all again, in the tent, behind my closed eyelids, and felt again that rush of resentment. Greenfield must have known she was coming here; why else his sly amusement at my surprise? He'd known, and not bothered to tell me, in his office, when I revealed my plans.

"I'm taking a week of my vacation right now, Charlie. It can't wait."

The swivel chair tilting back with a screech, the long, searching look. I waited for his customary indignation at being deprived of a vital cog in his life-support system, but it was not forthcoming. No caustic reproach, no specious arguments against the plan, no long-suffering resignation. Just, rather debonairly, "Funny, I never thought of you as capricious."

"It's not caprice, it's asphyxiation. Anyway, Stewart can handle the story on the zoning battle."

Two weeks earlier, he would have said, "Stewart will not bring me a story, he'll bring me a twenty-page tome on the history of social inequity." This time, merely a wry look.

"I'm going to Hunegger."

The quilled eyebrows rose up his forehead. "You're asphyxiating and you're going to Hunegger." He seemed amused. "Another esoteric symbiosis: futile protest as a sure cure for suffocation."

And good-bye. Not a word about who else had gone off to Hunegger. And now *she* knew he hadn't told me. I'd given her that, on a platter.

Worn out with the combination of a long, full day and injured pride, I finally slept, until a sound woke me: a patter of light rain on the tent. Handfuls of tiny drops, like someone sprinkling the ironing. Oh Lord, rain. Stiffly, I raised myself and looked out through the netting. It was dawn. Gray-green mist, the woods beyond the meadow all but invisible. A fresh, innocent smell of clean wet grass. No one stirring out there.

With a variety of contortions I wouldn't have thought possible, I got into my slicker, gathered clothes, soap dish and towel, wondering how the latter would ever dry, stuffed them under the slicker and crawled out into the wet mist.

The ablutionary amenities in the long trailer were elementary, and the combined odors of stale soap, damp wood and disinfectant were hardly calculated to raise the spirit. Posh by comparison, were we? I wouldn't have lasted twenty minutes at Greenham. Somewhat washed, I was rubbing myself dry when JoAnne entered, her pale, freckled cheeks misted, her straight hair plastered down by the rain like a cap of antique brass.

"Well, hello, a fellow early riser. Don't you love being up before the world gets used? My father, poor soul, used to say"—her voice fell to a turgid baritone—" 'Dawn is fine, for those that don't imbibe. But I—am not a member of that tribe.' Bed, book, and bottle was Daddy's idea of a good time." Humming, she leaned over the sink and proceeded to splash and scrub vigorously. "Harriet says you're a reporter."

"Not while I'm here. I told her I was here to help, not to report on it. I'm on Security. I have a meeting with Doris at ten."

"We might have to recruit you, though, in your other capacity."

"What for?"

"Come around to the barn."

An hour later I was sitting on an old kitchen chair, a Styrofoam cup of pretty bad coffee from a huge thermos in my hand. JoAnne lay full length on the bench. Harriet perched on another chair, behind the desk, the network of lines on her face showing clearly in the glare from the unshaded bulb overhead. Intrepid Lotte sat cross-legged on the floor, hands on knees, a back to make a ramrod seem flaccid. Doris in her blue glasses rested her solid rear against the table edge, arms folded.

"You're the only one here," Harriet was saying to me, "who has legitimate credentials."

"But if it's a press conference," I said, "it'll be public knowledge tomorrow. You can read it in the paper."

"No offense," said Doris, offensively, "but press reports are usually inaccurate and *never* comprehensive."

"We'll read what she said," JoAnne pointed out, "but not what she *didn't* say. If you hear both the questions and the answers, you'll have some idea of what she's holding back."

"And, of course, you can ask your own questions." Harriet's small, private smile lurked at the corners of her mouth. "*Our* questions."

"Such as?"

"Well, for instance—" JoAnne sipped coffee and wrinkled her nose. "—for instance, Alice Dakin has an organization, she has an office, she has staff, back in her hometown, in Kansas."

"Iowa," Doris said instantly.

"Missouri," said Harriet. "She moved."

JoAnne waved a hand. "Out there in the American heartland, where she's busy clogging up the American arteries. Anyway, in her headquarters, one assumes, she has lists of sympathizers in different parts of the country; organizations and/or individuals she can count on to assemble the local talent when they get the word she's coming to town. It would be good to know who, in Hunegger or Padua, is on her coordinating committee."

Doris moved impatiently. "This is going to take too long. We have to find a way to get her out of here. She's not going to waste any time; before you know it she'll have everybody in this town out for our blood. Some of them are bad enough as it is. All they need is that number one bitch telling them we're a bunch of perverts and coke sniffers."

"So this is the question," Lotte spoke up from the floor, "how we are going to stop this person. Maybe she's breaking the law?"

"It's not against the law," Doris said, "to stage a counterdemonstration. All you need is a permit."

"Of course," I said, "if you could convince the police that a confrontation would result in bodily harm . . ."

JoAnne shook her head. "We couldn't prove it. *Our* demonstrators aren't even here yet, the majority of them. How do you prove that a group of undetermined character confronting a provocateur group of undetermined character is going to result in anything more than shouting?"

"I say dump her in the river." Doris, scowling, looked capable of it. "Take her out in the woods and lose her."

JoAnne got up to refill her coffee cup. "How would you get past that honor guard she carries with her? And even if you could, she wouldn't stay lost long enough."

"How long do you want her lost?" Doris demanded.

JoAnne lay down again. "Forever sounds nice."

Lotte laughed, a short bark. "Dreams. Dreams."

Harriet said, "Let's be practical. The first thing we have to do is to find out as much as possible about her intentions and her setup. Maggie's in the best position to do that."

The barn door creaked, footfalls thudded on the floorboards, and a figure in a loden-green poncho appeared, her hair glowing against the dimness of the day. I fought a reflexive surge of adrenaline.

"A cabal if ever I saw one!" Heath-Morecomb's clipped

syllables rang like chimes in the murky morning. "You look like a scene from *Richard the Third*. Who's for the tower?"

"That's what we need," JoAnne said, "a tower."

"I sense complications."

Doris told her about Alice Dakin.

"Ah! And this Dakin—I gather she's within shooting distance?"

"*There's* a thought." JoAnne blew on her coffee. "She's staying at the Sycamore. Genghis Khan buttons for sale in the lobby."

"And she's come to disrupt the proceedings. Ai! Ai! Ai! Well, we'll have to think of it as a challenge. But first, I'm going to need some canvas. About two hundred feet of it. And some gaffer tape and phosphorescent paint. Also I'm going to need volunteers for taping and painting. And an advance scout to send into the base tonight. Maggie, you'd do admirably for that."

"Into the *base*?" I got up, looking for escape.

"Just the person. Trained observer, good memory, resourceful . . ."

"I've already got a job," I said quickly, and retreated from the room, the barn, and the camp.

With more than an hour to fill before the Dakin "press conference," I drove into Padua in search of a shopping center: a reporter should, at the very least, have a notebook. Padua was scrupulously clean, well kept, with wide, tree-shaded streets, and freshly painted turn-of-the-century houses, with deep front porches, sitting fatly behind spacious lawns. There was a pristine apartment complex in new buff-colored brick, an imposing courthouse fronted by Ionic columns—and very few people. The place looked as though it had been spruced up for a charity drive and nobody'd come. I drove into an all but deserted shopping mall. Where on earth was the populace? Surely they couldn't *all* work at the base?

In a supermarket I found not only a notebook but a salad bar, and decided to risk spoilage by filling a container with greens and beans, beets and olives, tomatoes and chick-peas, for consumption as soon as possible after leaving the Dakin doings: the breakfast of thin coffee and one slice of jam-smeared toast was not going to sustain me for long.

On the way to the Sycamore Inn it occurred to me to hope Greenfield would never learn how I was spending my time as an activist. I could just hear the quiet, incisive comment: "Obviously, your taking notes in Padua instead of Sloan's Ford has brought the world infinitely closer to nuclear disarmament." Something like that.

Assuming, of course, that he was himself again, and not the weird, lighthearted, bird-feeder-watching absentee editor of recent days. I fantasized coming home to find a fully recovered Greenfield. It was possible—just possible —that my leaving had shocked him back to normalcy. Should I call him? No, let him stew. Let him imagine me scaling the chain link fence of the base, being gunned down by armed police. . . .

The base. What was this scheme of Heath-Morecomb's that needed advance scouts sneaking onto the base at night? Could she possibly be serious? They did things like that at Greenham, I recalled. Invading the control tower. Good God. I found myself reluctantly admitting a certain respect for Heath-Morecomb's daring.

The misty rain had stopped—or paused—by the time I reached the entrance to the Sycamore Inn. There were no buttons for sale in the lobby, but a gaggle of people milled about, including several self-important young men with the unmistakable thrusting chins and ceaselessly vigilant eyes of staff aides. A couple of tape recorders identified a small group of newshounds lounging near the entrance to the dining room. Among the motley remainder I noticed a familiar face: the woman from the class of '54 in the uncreasable pale blue suit who had characterized the pro-testers as terrorist screwballs. No particular surprise to find her here.

When the group with the tape recorders moved into the

dining room, I followed. Greenfield had once, in a fit of conventionality, had *Reporter* cards printed, and I presented one to the earnest young woman at the entrance, who checked it against a list and looked uncertain. Before she could do more than hesitate, I gave her a confident smile and walked briskly to one of the chairs set in a semicircle around a cleared area in the center of the room. A half-dozen of us sat there ignoring one another until a rather small, fortyish woman, in a powdery pink silk dress, crossed the room with quick, ladylike steps and sat down facing us, at a table holding a water jug and a glass.

"I'm Alice Dakin," she said in a thin, girlish voice. "Thank you for coming. I think we all know why I'm here." She smiled quickly, without parting her lips. The smile was programmed for one second and it didn't last a fraction longer. "It's my belief, and I think all loyal Americans agree with me, that one of the greatest dangers we face at this time is not from outside forces, but from those within our own country who want to leave us weak and defenseless in the face of the overwhelming threat from communist countries." She cleared her throat politely. "These terribly misguided people are planning a demonstration here this coming weekend in an effort to give the impression that the American people are opposed to our nuclear strike force. *We* are here—and many more of us will be here this weekend—to show the world just how false that impression is. The *majority*—of the American people—believe that God wants *our* country to *survive*. And that He gave us the knowledge to create nuclear weapons so that we *would* survive."

I wondered how Einstein would have felt about God getting all the credit. Not to mention that other God, whoever He was, who gave the same knowledge to the Soviets.

"Now if there are any questions, I'll be glad to answer them."

A batch of standard questions ensued. How many supporters did she expect to show up. Were they planning a march. Would she be making any speeches. How long was she planning to stay in the area. Did she expect trouble from the Women's Peace Camp. All her replies somehow managed to include the fact that God was on the side of Alice Dakin and her supporters, and if the rest of the world had to be wiped out to prove it, that was an unfortunate consequence of its intransigence. Nowhere did she allow for the fact that "her" country might need more than a few Band-Aids as a result of God's partiality.

I worded my question to make evasion seem rude. "Would you like to make any mention of the particular local citizens who've given their time and effort to help you organize things in the Hunegger Base area?"

She gestured to one of the stuffy young men I'd seen in the lobby, a plump, perspiring one in limp seersucker straining against its buttons. He handed her a typed list, and reading from it, she reeled off the names of the half-dozen locals who'd been happy to assist, praised the cooperation of the county supervisor, the city police and the sheriff's office, and mentioned the local radio talk-show host who would be interviewing her later in the day. I asked if she would be attending any social functions while she was here.

"I didn't come here to socialize," she piped. "However, I have one or two friends in the area and I imagine I'll be invited to dinner." A flick of a smile accompanied this, indicating that it was humor.

"Friends at the base, you mean?"

She ignored this and nodded at a tired man sitting three chairs away who looked as though he might be a stringer for an Albany paper.

Friends at the base, I wrote. *No names, ranks or serial numbers. Air Force not to be associated with any demonstration, con or pro.*

When the questions finally trailed off, she thanked us again for coming, granted us one last closed-mouth smile, and clicked daintily out of the room. I watched her go, a small, shrewd, well-rehearsed package who'd been born understanding politics; if you can help it, never answer the question that's been asked.

I was hungry. I went out to the car, wolfed down the aging salad I'd left on the seat in its foil container with the plastic fork, and longed for something hot, liquid, and palatable. I drove into Hunegger, telling myself that unpromising places like the Mills Café often served surprisingly good coffee.

If anything, it was worse than the camp's. I left a half cup to the investigating nose of a greedy cat slinking around among the Formica tables with their paper place mats, and started back to the camp.

As I crossed the small iron bridge I'd crossed with Brenda the night before, a splash of tangerine color on the grassy bank of the stream below made me pull off the road and stop to admire. Wild daylilies, an entire corps de ballet of them, bright petals swaying on the ends of long, graceful stalks, covered a stretch of bank just beyond a bend in the stream where trees and bushes grew down to the water's edge. The overhanging branches of the trees cast dim, feathery reflections in the placid, winding stream. The bushes followed the bank's curves with that harmonious felicity only natural contours can achieve. It was a small pastoral gem and profoundly peaceful.

I wondered how far this little stream meandered. It disappeared behind a thick growth of dark green vegetation on the Hunegger side, and on the other it wandered quietly off in the direction of the camp. I was tempted to abandon the car and follow it on foot. A little serenity for the spirit, a little loveliness for the eye to dwell on . . . I started the car and drove on to make my report to the cabal. Much good it would do them to learn what I'd been able to discover.

CHAPTER FIVE

BRENDA CAME AROUND THE SIDE OF THE BARN AS I drove up the track and parked. She came to meet me. "The tent was leaking," she said, brandishing a roll of adhesive tape. "You ever open your eyes at four in the morning and find water dripping on your face and no place to get away from it? I woke up the roommates and said what do you say we take turns sleeping under the leak? They didn't go for it. I had to lug my sleeping bag into the barn and use the floor in the front office. When Doris found me there this morning she gave me a lecture. I'm lying there in a damp sleeping bag feeling like twenty kinds of shit and she's lecturing me."

"These are the times that try an activist's soul," I agreed, and we went into the barn together. Brenda returned the adhesive to the so-called infirmary, a cubbyhole with a locked medicine chest and a cot, while I walked in, apparently, on a conference in the office where Harriet and JoAnne presided. With Doris and Lotte they huddled around the secondhand desk, looking intense and speaking in lowered voices, but at my entrance they broke off abruptly and leaned away from each other.

"You have a message," Harriet said, reaching into a mail slot and handing me a slip of paper.

Greenfield! I thought triumphantly. Wrong: Elliot. An olive branch! I thought, with relief. Wrong again. *Called out to the Tulsa job. Office has the number. Two or three days. George with the Olivers. Take care.* Not much room there for interpretation. If I'd been around to get the call, I might have been able to tell his mood from his voice. Alice Dakin had much to answer for.

I put the message in my pocket and reported on the Dakin press party. JoAnne, elbows on the desk, hands cupping her chin, stared at the far wall. Doris trained her glasses on the floor. Lotte sat on the edge of the desk, slowly raising and lowering her legs. Harriet, with that faint, amiable smile on her lips, was the only one who looked at me while I talked.

I gave them my impressions and a more or less verbatim account of the proceedings, and handed over my notes, including the names of the locals who had assisted the Dakin staff.

"Sounds like she has an army coming," Doris said.

"Funding's probably good," JoAnne reminded her. "She could probably bus them in from all over the Northeast."

"We block the road," Lotte suggested, "lie down on the road, let nobody pass."

"Except our people," Harriet pointed out. "And how will we know which are our people and which are theirs? They're not going to be wearing team suits."

"We tell ours to wear something."

"There's no time," Doris said, taking it seriously, "and

even if there were, I can just see Slater letting us get away with it."

"I know this isn't going to be a popular point of view," I put in, "but it seems to me ignoring her is the best bet. I don't see how she can be stopped, and making a fuss only escalates her importance. She may even be *hoping* for interference. Gives her free publicity and injures our credibility."

They received the unsolicited advice first with silence, then with those indistinct murmurs and throat clearings that signify a decision to the contrary has already been made and nobody wants to discuss it further.

"Anyway," JoAnne said, pouncing on the notes, "this is all very useful, Maggie. You've done a magnificent job, which doesn't surprise me at all because I pegged you instantly as clever and quick."

Right, I thought—now, if I could only play the violin.

I departed the meeting in the company of Doris, who took me to the front office, where she gave me a whistle and a walkie-talkie and asked if I'd brought a flashlight.

"Yes. The batteries are going, though."

She gave me some batteries from a box on a shelf and took me outside to explain the security procedure. "You'll be on with Mariko, second shift, midnight to four. She'll cover the barn, the latrine, and the first section of tents. You start at the kitchen shack and go back from there, the whole second camping area and the grounds as far as the tree line. You see anything suspicious, get on the walkie-talkie. You run into trouble, blow the whistle, it's a pretty loud whistle, nobody's going to sleep through that."

"How deep are those woods?"

"At the back, pretty deep. On the left, just about twenty feet, then you're on somebody's property. On the right they thin out pretty quick, there's a river going through there."

"A river!"

"A small one, a stream. Okay? Any questions? One of the girls on the first shift will come wake you up at twelve, and when you're finished you wake up Cynthia in tent fourteen."

"Cynthia?"

"A black woman. A Ph.D. from Harvard."

I nodded. Second shift, the worst one. On the first shift there would still be campers around for at least half of it. On the last, you'd get two hours of early light. I wondered if it was policy to break in the new people with the toughest job. Doris went briskly back into the barn. It would be nice, I thought, if all the people with whom you were in sympathy were sympathetic people. So far the ratio was fifty-fifty.

I put the whistle and the walkie-talkie in among my clothes in the tent, and set out for a walk around the campgrounds. I'd been doing too much sitting. A stream, Doris said, through the trees on the right. Could it be that same lovely stream that ran under the bridge in Hunegger? Would there be orange daylilies on the bank? I headed for the trees.

There was a moss-green gloom among the trees and a smell of decomposing leaves from the ground. Between the tree trunks I caught a glimpse of tall wild grass ahead and after a minute or so the gloom lightened, the trees thinned, and there was the stream. A little wider than it was where it flowed under the Hunegger bridge—if indeed it was the same stream—but just as peaceful. I walked along the bank, watching the quiet flow of the olive-green water, wondering what magic it was that gave a body of water the power to heal, just by its existence. A stream, a lake, a harbor, the sea. How people flocked to the seaside. How sailors yearned to set sail. Was it because water was the one thing on earth man hadn't—so far—been able to cover with asphalt? For the first time in weeks, I felt calm. It was lovely to be alone, and quiet, near the water.

I rounded a bend where the trees and brush grew thickly. Just ahead, an enormous, venerable willow hung softly over the bank, its foliage so thick and its lower branches so near the ground that the wands caressed the grass around its entire circumference, forming a feathery, yellow-green curtain around the trunk. A sort of verdant hoopskirt, a circular willow tent. I smiled.

And heard a voice, from inside the enveloping willow. A man's voice.

A man? On the campgrounds? In the trees? I moved, soundlessly, closer.

The voice was deep and quiet. Intimate, teasing. "Why? Because it's my job. There *are* people like me. It's a fact of life. I'm not one of your crazies. I shouldn't even be here. With you. You're nothing but trouble. You know that, don't you. . . . Well? . . . Don't just smile, talk to me. . . . One way or another . . . talk to me."

I turned back and very carefully retraced my steps.

Well, I thought, that's what riverbanks were for, among other things. Obviously not a security matter. In any case, I wasn't going to report it. A little splendor in the grass was par for this time of year.

I followed the stream in the opposite direction for a half mile or so, turned and walked back to a point that seemed reasonably close to where I'd originally entered the trees, and returned to the meadow. There would be a workshop going on shortly in the barn, concerning nonviolent civil disobedience. I should attend: I'd already missed the orientation session that morning. But the prospect of sitting in one of those cubicles discussing what to do when arrested was dismal to the point of serious depression. I admired my fellow campers, I certainly shared their abhorrence of nuclear weapons, but I was not, essentially, a team player. Besides, I had no intention of being arrested.

I crawled into my tent. I would sit there and conscientiously read all the literature I'd been handed since I'd arrived. Perhaps I'd learn there all I needed to know. I learned very little, got as far as community responsibility in leafletting and garbage disposal, and fell asleep. Brenda woke me.

"Hey!" she said.

I sat up. Was it morning, noon, night? Where was the

missile I'd just stolen from a B52 and defused by wrapping it in colored yarn I'd taken from the now stringless violin lying on the water of the meandering stream? I looked at my watch. Two hours had gone.

"What?" I said.

"H.-M. wants you."

"What's H.-M.?"

"The redhead."

H.-M. Of course. Her Majesty. "What do you mean, *wants* me?" *Her Majesty wants the Captain of the Guards, wants the chauffeur, wants the upstairs maid.*

Brenda struggled to convey Heath-Morecomb's actual words, but her attempt at a British accent was so unintelligible I gathered only that the woman was in the barn. I visited what Doris, in her unvarnished way, referred to as the latrine, splashed my face with icy water from the sink, and went to the barn. There was no one in the front office. I opened the door into the barn proper and found, just beyond the threshold, stretching the full length of the barn, a carpet of uncolored canvas. Kneeling on it, twenty feet apart, were two young women laboriously stretching silver-backed tape across its surface. A closer look revealed that what lay on the floor actually consisted of three long strips of canvas, each about five feet wide and twenty feet long, and the girls were taping the three long strips to each other.

A banner for the march? If so, they'd *need* a thousand demonstrators, just to carry it.

At the far end of the barn, Heath-Morecomb was on her hands and knees taking measurements with a ruler and making marks on the canvas.

"Seven words," she was saying. "Twenty-six letters in all. Two spaces between each word, two each at the beginning and the end, sixteen spaces, that's a total of forty-two. Two hundred divided by forty-two is . . . well, it's roughly five. Four point seven and a bit. Therefore . . . we have to scrimp a little on each five feet."

"How do I get in?" I called.

She looked up, the fire of her hair quenched by the straw boater she was wearing again, minus the kitschy hatband. "Oh, Maggie. Good. You can walk on the canvas, we haven't painted yet."

"And when you have, I fly?" I covered the distance on foot.

"You have no idea"—she stood up—"what Sisyphean labor it was, tracking down this canvas. Would you consider it possible that this area, once the textile center of the universe, or thereabouts, should be down, virtually, to its last bolt of natural canvas? Moved out, all the mills, the lot of them. All gone down South, where the captive labor abounds. And gaffer's tape—never heard of it! Now, that's a term commonly used on this side of the Atlantic: having served my time as the wife of a man-of-the-theatah, I know whereof I speak. But you'd think I was asking for plover's eggs in Iceland. Finally had to sort through the man's dusty shelves with my own hands to find it. 'That's *duck* tape,' he says. *Duck!* What in hell do *ducks* have to do with it?"

"Duct," I said, courtesy of Elliot, "as in plumbing pipes." *Man of the theater. So, she was somebody's wife. Or had been.* "I hear you were looking for me."

"Yes, about tonight, the reconnaissance—"

"I don't think I volunteered."

"Now, look here, are you *with* us, or merely observing?"

"What's the reconnaissance for?"

"We're going to take in a message and leave it there. It will not detonate, nor will it cause harm to any living thing."

"Who's *we?*"

"Five of us."

"Why don't one of you do the reconnaissance?"

"We're all going to be working our little fannies off up to the last minute. What I want you to do is this—"

"There are at least fifty women camping out there. Pick someone else."

"My dear, we may all be equally worthy, but we are not all equally endowed. *You* I have chosen. Now, once you're on the base—"

"Assuming it's even possible—"

"Of course it's possible. A four-strand barbed-wire fence. A *child* could get into that base."

"A very thin child."

"That's what wire clippers are for."

Wire clippers! "I may not have mentioned it," I said, "but I've always felt a terrific disinclination to trespass on federal property. What I feel about *damaging* federal property is more in the nature of paralysis."

She looked at me and began to swing the ruler in her hand like a pendulum. "Tell me something. *Why*—did you come to the peace camp?"

She would have had to be the entire KGB holding electric prods to get that answer out of me.

"Not to mess with the law," I said.

She lifted the ruler with two fingers, let it drop to the floor, and said with a quiet sneer, "Good God, woman, is your moral outrage confined to what's *comfortable?*"

All right, then, the gloves were off. "If it were," I managed to say, "I wouldn't be here! I'm not *comfortable* here. I'm not *comfortable* coming face-to-face with potential extinction, looking at that fence every day, knowing what's behind it. I'm not *comfortable* knowing we're about to confront that Dakin woman and her belligerent followers, I won't be *comfortable* at three o'clock in the morning patrolling the camp looking for hostile interlopers with knives!"

She smiled. *"C'est magnifique,* Maggie, *mais ce n'est pas la guerre."*

"It's not going to make a fraction of difference to the *guerre,* if I get arrested. Frankly, I think this business of deliberately climbing over fences into the arms of the police only trivializes the whole protest. It comes off as adolescent bravado."

"Well, you're wrong, of course. The only protest that's

64

ineffectual is the one nobody knows about. As long as we're in the public eye we're having an effect. *Any*thing we can do, short of violence, to focus attention on the issue is important. *I've* been arrested. My *daughter's* been arrested. This is not the Beaux Arts Ball, nor is it the playing fields of Eton, though I understand a lot of dirty stuff went on in both places. Now I'm running out of time, are you going to help?"

So she had a daughter.

"How old is your daughter?"

"Twenty-four. She arrived when *I* was twenty-four. You don't need a calculator for that—and I would like to see *her* daughter, and her *daughter's* daughter also arrive at suitable intervals. So let's get on with it, we have a lot of work to do."

I'VE been arrested. The coup de grâce.

I gave her a hard look and turned away. "I think I should take someone with me. How about Brenda?"

CHAPTER SIX

LIPPED *ONE STRAND* OF BARBED WIRE,"
Heath-Morecomb repeated in disgust. "Bloody marvel-
ous!" She spun the wheel of the Ford Escort and the car
obediently made a right turn into a lane of opposing traffic.
Fortunately the only opposing traffic was a quarter of a
mile away and she corrected the mistake before it arrived.
Easy to see why the first car had "collapsed": the strain
of knowing it was constantly on the wrong side of the
road. From the back seat I heard Brenda and JoAnne
expel the breath they'd been holding.

In the front passenger seat, I fumed. I was in no mood
for imperial contempt. Brenda and I had been apprehended, we had been handcuffed, we had been carted
off to the security police building, herded into a room to
have the "flexicuffs" cut off our abraded wrists, then into

another room where a Major Somebody with a head cold had read us our rights and charged us with trespassing. We'd been fingerprinted, photographed, frightened into near imbecility, and finally released with a formal warning that we were henceforth barred from the base. That might not call for medals to be struck, but disdain, in my estimation, was pushing it. My response to Heath-Morecomb's *bloody mahvlous* was less than conciliatory.

"Somehow," I said, "when I weighed three years in a prison cell against a passion for headlines, the choice was easy."

"Women have died," she said, "and worms have eaten them, but not for clipping a fence. No one gets three years for *clipping.*" She made another quick turn, this time into the correct lane, but on only two of the four wheels provided. "The whole point of the exercise was for you to *simplify* things for us. *Find* the closest access and *open—it—up.* So that *five* of us, carrying a very large, very bulky object, could get in and out of that base within fifteen minutes. Now you've not only given us the three remaining strands of barbed wire to contend with, but a lovely little game of who-can-find-the-wire-cutters-in-the-dark."

"The ladder will be there," Brenda insisted from the back seat, "where we left it."

JoAnne, beside her, said, "Not if they've been checking the fence," her normally liquid voice rigid with tension. "Now, they may be damn fools, but you *know* they're going to do that."

"At night?" I said. "Fourteen miles of fence? And besides, they think we came in near the front gate."

"You *told* them you came in that way," Heath-Morecomb corrected. "What they *believe* is between them and their God. It won't have escaped their attention that you couldn't identify the place when they took you back."

I remembered the confused, uncertain expressions Brenda and I had assumed as we pretended, for the benefit of the unsmiling young military policeman, to search for the spot where we'd entered.

"It was right before that clump of trees."

"No, it was *after* the trees, farther down, near the other trees."

"I don't know, trees all look alike to me—"

"In the dark, you know—"

Had he believed us?

I looked out the window at the indistinct boundary of the base flashing by. "We'll know soon enough. Slow down a little, we're almost there." I recognized the row of single-family homes on the right, saw the Honda parked up ahead. With a lurch of fear, I realized the police had seen my driver's license: would they have checked to find out what car I drove, in spite of my lie that I'd left the car at home and the fact that I had no keys on me? Would they have scoured the perimeter roads looking for it? Were they lying in ambush, waiting for me to come and retrieve it?

"Here," I said. "The third house down is where the ladder belongs, if you get out of the base alive."

Heath-Morecomb drew to the side of the road and shut off the ignition.

"The ladder's up there," Brenda said, pointing, "near a big tree next to the fence."

Heath-Morecomb got out of the car quietly, Brenda opened the rear door and climbed out, almost quietly, followed by JoAnne, and the three of them crossed the road. I left the car and went down the road to the Honda, the skin between my shoulder blades prickling in anticipation of a tap on the shoulder as I took the keys from under the fender and opened the door. If the MPs were waiting for me, they were taking their time about coming to get me. I slid under the wheel and crouched down. No one came out of the dark to shine a flashlight in my face.

I peered through the rear window, wondering what was happening. Then I saw H.-M. crossing to the Ford and Brenda coming toward me. She opened the door and got in beside me.

"Ladder's still there," she said, breathless, "JoAnne's

going to stay with it and H.-M.'s going back to collect the others, with the stuff."

The "stuff" was the huge strip of canvas I'd seen Heath-Morecomb measuring on the barn floor earlier in the day. After Brenda and I had been escorted to the main gate by the military police, and released, and had trotted a mile and a half back to the camp to arrive at the barn breathless and quivering, the "stuff" was still on the barn floor, but rolled up now, like a carpet for a very long corridor. Standing around it were the five women who were going to smuggle it onto the base, and while I reported on the fence, the runway, the security cop and all the rest of it, one end of the "stuff" came free from the roll and fell flat to reveal an enormous letter T painted in phosphorescent red on the pale canvas. H.-M.'s "message" seemed like a lot of trouble to go to for an episode that wasn't likely to reverberate in the public mind for more than twenty-four hours. Trouble *and* risk.

"It's true," I said, "they don't have a permanent patrol there, the way they do in the Alert area, but that cop could be driving by on a regular basis. Particularly now that we've been picked up."

They'd looked at me as though I hadn't a clue to the meaning of activism.

I started the car.

"So where are we going?" Brenda was still breathless, perhaps permanently.

"We were told to be visible." What Heath-Morecomb had actually said was, "Now that you have a *bar* letter," referring to the formal warning that banned us from the base as though it were a failing grade in some exam, "I suggest you spend the next hour or so in town, preferably where people will see you and remember you. You won't want to be suspected of a second trespass."

"I could use a drink," Brenda said. "I wonder if it's okay for peaceniks to hang out in the local saloon."

"We're not only peaceniks," I reminded her, "we're what they call 'unaccompanied females.' In Manhattan that may no longer have overtones, but up here we might just find ourselves with customers."

"After what we've been through, what've we got to lose?"

We headed for Padua, approaching it from the northern outskirts, a route I'd never traveled before. A dark, residential avenue lined with maples and chestnuts led us into a wide main road devoted to commerce: real estate offices, convenience stores, an automobile showroom, all set far back from the road behind paved parking areas, all new, shiny, banal, and, of course, shut dead. The streets were empty of human traffic. I despaired of finding anything so inviting as a neighborhood tavern alive with people.

The avenue, however, eventually debouched into a narrower street of century-old buildings, separated from the roadway only by shallow, patched sidewalks, and there, between an abandoned factory and a meager shopfront advertising TV repairs, was a sight to gladden the heart. I pulled into the curb and we sat there, incredulous, grinning at the peeling and rusted wrought-iron marquee attached to the nineteenth-century façade that grandly announced: THE PLAZA.

"The *Plaza!*" Brenda choked. "The *Plaza.*"

From behind the tall, wide, mullioned windows with their stone lintels shone a warm, amber light. In one of the windows glowed a small, anomalous neon sign: BAR. Brenda leaped from the car and sashayed to the entrance, swinging from the waist down: her shorts were a satin gown and her dirty sneakers the gin-soaked sandals of Zelda Fitzgerald.

I followed her across the stone doorstep and into a high, narrow lobby with a tiled floor, the walls wood-paneled for the first six feet, ochre plaster from there up, and, shedding the amber light, a chandelier of branched tulip shapes that might have been the first one to shine down on Tom Edison's parlor. At the far end a dim, uncarpeted staircase with a wooden banister ascended to the upper regions, where, I felt certain, the ghosts of traveling salesmen still hefted their sample cases of hair tonic and ladies' corsets onto narrow iron beds.

"This is bi*zarre,*" Brenda said. "Must have been built in the Civil War."

"Not quite, but at least while Scarlett could still hobble around."

We pursued the sounds of amiable banter through an archway into another long, narrow room, where thirty feet of burnished mahogany bar was backed by a mirror the size of a small pond that hung between tooled wooden pillars. One could spend a year, I thought, speculating on the changing faces and costumes that glass had reflected over the past century or so.

At the moment it reflected several paunchy, cheerful men and two younger, tired ones, one with a moustache, sitting on the high wood stools nursing their beers, and a stout, moist-eyed matron who kept raising her glass in a solemn toast to someone called Nick. The younger men, I realized, were the avid filmmakers who'd been arguing with JoAnne at the camp. Behind the bar a short, moon-faced man with eyes like black olives gave us a friendly smile, a "vodka on ice with a twist" for Brenda, and a sherry for me. No sidelong glances, I noted, either lewd or censorious. Apparently *unaccompanied females* were not necessarily pigeonholed at this bar.

"Sherry?" Brenda said, wrinkling her nose at my glass.

"Didn't you know?" I invented. "Sherry is in. Vodka is out. White wine is out. All of Madison Avenue is drinking sherry. It's a return to old values."

She looked skeptical.

"Here's to Nick," the stout woman intoned. "He never hurt a fly."

We drank to being safely off the base. We drank to the speedy return of the other five. Brenda and the moustache eyed each other. The other men eyed Brenda's legs wistfully. The man behind the bar pushed a tiny plate of peanuts in my direction, beaming, and asked how we were making out down at the camp.

"What makes you think we're from the camp?"

"What makes me think? I grew up in this town. My family's been running this hotel for sixty-three years. If you came from around here, I'd know you." He crinkled his black eyes at me and went off to pour another beer.

That's not the whole story, I thought. We could be tourists, we could be on our way to some other town. No, we must carry a mark, the look of people who sleep on the ground and groom themselves in a latrine.

Brenda, possibly bearing in mind that we were there to be remembered, also possibly showing off for the benefit of the moustache, got up and danced, solo, to some incomprehensible song from a radio behind the bar, while the men looked on, gratified. Live entertainment, at no extra price.

"Give you the shirt off his back, Nick." The stout woman's eyes were brimming. "A lovely, lovely person."

"Where is he?" Brenda called out. "Where's Nick? I want to meet him."

The woman stared at her. "He's at the vet," she said. "Worms."

It was past eleven when I yawned and suddenly remembered. "Damn! I meant to get some sleep! I'm on sentry duty or whatever they call it!"

We paid up, promised Julius-whose-family-had-run-the-Plaza-for-sixty-three-years that we would return someday soon to take lunch or dinner in the dining room across the lobby, and drove back to the camp along the dark, quiet roads.

"His name's Michael," she said.

"Who?"

"The one with the moustache. He's an independent filmmaker. He's got an in with PBS. He borrowed the equipment. It's video."

"Mm."

"Wonder if they made it," Brenda mused. "JoAnne and the rest of them. You think they made it? You think they got picked up? What do you think?"

"Think! I can barely drive."

At the camp the barn was deserted except for one of the girls on the first security shift checking through it. I asked if she'd seen Harriet or any of the others, she said no, but the sign was up on the loft, that meant someone was up there, sleeping. I borrowed her flash, went to the ladder that led to the loft and shone the light upward. There was a sign hung by a string on a nail in the support beam: DO NOT DISTURB. My eyes felt heavy. I gave back the flash and dragged myself after Brenda, out of the barn and across the grass, Brenda dancing ahead of me, caroling "Twelve bells and all's well! Rest easy, girls, we're gonna be guarded by a sloshed-out zombie who can't keep her eyes open!"

I crawled once again into my claustrophobe's nightmare: seventeen minutes left for a sound, refreshing sleep. I lay down, closed my eyes, and the events of the evening immediately began to pass in review. I saw, again, that row of giant B52s, so patient, so powerful, so pregnant with death. I saw the high chain link fence around the Alert area and the airman with the rifle, the dim outline of the hangar as we skulked through the dark toward the runway. I felt again the shock of turning to see that large uniformed presence blocking our retreat, the security guard, an odd man, that faintly humorous expression, something about him that didn't fit, something out of context, bothersome, disturbing. . . .

A voice, pitched low, came through the netting of the fly. "You Maggie?"

"Yes?"

"You're on."

"Oh. Right. Thanks." I dug out my whistle and my walkie-talkie and crawled out into the night.

A three-quarter moon, pale as a slice of cucumber with a bite missing, rode in and out of cloud as though searching for the piece it had lost. The air seemed warmer than it had earlier, almost balmy: perhaps it was the sherry. I switched on the flash and went in search of my partner.

Always advisable to make friends with someone on whom you might have to rely for assistance.

Across the field a light flashed in the first area of tents. I made my way over to it and found the delicate little Oriental girl I'd seen at the main gate when I'd first arrived. Yum-Yum. Mariko. The other half of the security team for the next four hours. I looked at this girl who was going to protect the camp against hefty intruders, who was going to come running to my aid if need be: a tiny, slender wisp of five-foot-nothing. It was like leaning on a daffodil.

"Mariko? I'm Maggie. I'm covering the other half."

"Oh yes? Very good. You have a whistle? Yes? Walkie-talkie?"

"I've got everything. Have you seen JoAnne? Or Doris? Harriet?"

"No. No one. All sleeping, I think."

"If you see any of them, let me know."

"Okay, I tell you. Okay? I see you later." She went off, noiselessly, on her rounds, flashing her light to left and right.

I re-crossed the field, began my tour of inspection with the lower left quadrant of my assigned territory, and proceeded, clockwise, until, at the end of an hour I was back where I'd begun. Twice I'd seen a figure moving through the dark and reached for my whistle, but the first one had belonged to a large girl called Sheila who was stumbling sleepily toward the latrine, and the second to Mariko, who had wisely brought me a container of coffee from the kitchen shack. Without it, I would surely, on one of my rest stops, have drifted off into slumber. Even with it, my eyes felt grainy and my wits scattered. I'd risen at dawn that morning after only a few hours' sleep, the afternoon catnap had only made things worse, and the evening had hardly been restful. I was, in short, a bit of a wreck.

Sipping the hot coffee, I trudged through my second round, wondering if any of the tents I circled as I went held the sleeping form of Lotte or Doris. Or were they, like JoAnne and Harriet, considered staff, and therefore allowed a cot in what used to be the hayloft of the barn? Heath-Morecomb, being a sort of activist professor by virtue of Greenham, was undoubtedly in the hayloft.

If they were back. Because DO NOT DISTURB, I realized, didn't guarantee anything. They might all be up there, or *one* of them might be; on the other hand they might have put up the sign the night before and neglected to take it down in the morning.

But of course they were back, had to be. It was a good three hours since we'd left them near the ladder. Fifteen minutes, she'd said. In and out. If things had gone wrong and they'd been caught, the camp would know about it. There was always a "support group" behind any direct action or civil disobedience, which was responsible for coming up with the bail. Someone would have told us.

I felt aggrieved. Damned cold-blooded of them to have gone off to bed before Brenda and I got back. *One* of them could have waited up to tell us how the mission had gone. We *had* participated, after all. At some cost, by the way. How sharper than a serpent's tooth it is, to have a thankless brain trust.

By the third hour I'd gone beyond the need for sleep, I was in that nervy, light-headed, intensely alert state that precedes total collapse. I saw shadowy figures everywhere, heard sounds that no dog had ever heard. The tiniest rustle of a leaf in the bordering woods, a berry dropping from a bush a mile away, had me whirling in my tracks, whistle at the ready. The woods were nightmarish. Patrolling along the perimeters of the camp, as far from that menacing blackness as the beam of the flashlight allowed, I suffered a surge of adrenaline every twenty feet. The night life among those trees was prodigious. Squirrels, I told myself. (Did squirrels sleep?) Raccoons. Notorious for being up till all hours. Owls. Bats. A fox. A man.

I must never tell Elliot about this, I decided, or the rest of my life would be spent investigating those mysterious thumps and crashes that occurred in any household in the dead of night; a picture fallen off the wall, George running in his sleep. Maybe. And maybe not. "*You're* the security patrol expert, *you* go."

A little before three-thirty I consulted my watch and began to be hopeful that I would actually live to the end of my shift. There hadn't been any movement in the camp for the last hour and a half, except for the flicker of Mariko's flashlight at the other end of the meadow. No one going to the john. (Or the "loo," as Heath-Morecomb called it. Or the "jane," as the militant feminists insisted, though what glory attached itself to that edifice escaped me.) No one kicking out at the wall of a tent. No scurrying, unidentifiable animal. My pulse had returned to normal, my head was relatively at peace, I felt that I would sleep restfully as soon as I got the chance. Even the terrors of the woods had become familiar, and I was calmly completing my last circuit of the dread area when the beam of my flashlight picked up something moving slowly ahead of me in the grass.

Hearts do stop. I felt mine stop.

The something was my size, and moving away from me. No camper would be in this area, there was nothing here but the black beginning of the woods. The heart that had stopped was racing now. I fumbled in my pocket for the whistle, and the figure turned to face me.

In the light from the flash the red hair looked pale. Heath-Morecomb.

I lowered the whistle, breathed deeply and crossed the grass toward her.

"Oh, it's you," she said. She looked feverish, her eyes glistened. She licked at her lips and gave a short laugh. "I couldn't sleep. I'm strung up."

"How did it go?" I asked.

"It—? Oh, fine. Piece of veritable cake."

"You didn't run into the cop."

". . . No. No." She looked away and smiled faintly. "No trouble."

"What did you do with the canvas?"

"Left it in the appropriate place, of course, and got ourselves out of there. We put the ladder back."

"I wish I'd known you were awake." My polite murmur was a touch poisonous. "Brenda and I were wondering whether or not you'd all been caught. No one bothered waiting up to tell us."

"Well, as you see, we survived." No apology, no explanation. She took a deep breath. "Lord, I'm tired. What time is it?"

"Three-thirty."

Softly she said, "That late!" and drifted off toward the barn without another word.

It was only when I'd turned my duties over to Cynthia in tent fourteen and gone, finally, into my space capsule to sleep, that it occurred to me to wonder why Heath-Morecomb was still dressed in the clothes she'd worn on the way to the base. If she'd had trouble sleeping and decided to take a walk, surely she would simply have put a sweater over her pajamas? Surely she didn't go to bed in those jeans, and that shirt?

CHAPTER SEVEN

BY NOON THE NEXT DAY THE CAMP WAS SEETHING with activity. I woke to the sounds of sawing and hammering, the revving of a truck's motor, the clank of a metal shovel on stone, the cries of the women working in the grounds around me. On my way to the washhouse I saw Brenda and four other members of the garden detail staking out a large plot near the back boundary, digging up the earth and turning it, preparing it for tomato vines, corn, runner beans, whatever it was they were going to grow with the help of Brenda, that agricultural genius from south of Canal Street.

Behind the barn another group was still working on the construction of the shelter for housing workshops and meetings. In the washhouse two girls were busy with pails, brushes and disinfectant. I silently vowed I would volunteer to blockade the base single-handed rather than risk that job.

Washed and dressed—lightweight denim pants, a light cotton shirt, the temperature had climbed into the seventies—I went to the barn to see if there was any coffee to be had. On the way, I passed an open-air meeting on outreach work in the community:

"If we show them respect, they'll respect us."

"You have to talk to them, but it isn't enough to talk, you have to listen to the feedback. Try to find out how they feel about things, as individuals. I mean, they're just people. It's not *Them* and *Us,* it's *all* of us."

"Hostility? Well maybe they're afraid. They don't know who we are, we're strangers, there are a lot of us, they don't know *what* we're going to do. We have to communicate. Break down the barriers."

I intercepted JoAnne and Harriet as they walked from the barn toward the parking lot, JoAnne reading a letter aloud: " 'I don't know if I'll be able to stick it out at the print shop all summer. Glynis knows zilch about art and Hersh is a cultural snob with sinusitis. But I'll certainly let you know before I go backpacking in Borneo. Not to worry, Mom, I am destined for great things. Love, Rob.' Now, really, is that a beautiful boy? How *are* you, Maggie?"

"How are *you* is more to the point, after last night?"

"Oh, it was fun," JoAnne said, circles under her eyes, and Harriet added, "No problem at all," though she looked extremely pale.

JoAnne unlocked a dusty Buick. "We're on our way to town for a meeting with Rudko, the town supervisor, and some other local officials."

"We have to reassure them," Harriet explained, "that the camp will be responsible for an orderly demonstration march this weekend." She slipped into the passenger seat.

JoAnne put the key in the ignition. "Rudko says it's not *us* they're worried about, but *the dangerous element this kind of major action is going to attract.* Meaning the marchers who are coming to join us. I think they're expecting some kind of composite monster horde—half terrorist bombers, half punks wearing heavy metal and roaring into town on motorcycles equipped with ghetto blasters."

I asked, "What did they say about the Dakin group?"

"Not a word," Harriet said.

"*Nothing?* But the Dakin horde isn't even in the realm of conjecture, it's real, she said so!"

"Never fear"—JoAnne started up the car.—"we'll raise the specter."

In the front office Doris was conducting a session on legal rights:

"You have to know your U.S. criminal code, especially sections 1361 and 1363. . . .

"Suppose you're arrested on a misdemeanor, usually they offer you R.O.R.—release on your own recognizance —and give you a D.A.T.—that's a desk appearance ticket . . . .

"If civil disobedience results in a trial or a hearing, you have a right to go pro se, that means to represent yourself instead of having some lawyer spouting a lot of legalese that has nothing to do with why you're there. You're there because of a very personal, political conviction, you have a right to try to explain your motives, it's your constitutional right, just make sure you know the proper legal procedure . . .

"If you prefer confrontation and noncooperation, if you refuse R.O.R. or bail, you're going to be detained. Now . . ."

I moved on.

The main office was afloat in scribbled paper, and noisy with the vocal contributions of a half-dozen excited women trying to organize the upcoming demonstration while accommodating the proposals of various special interest groups. Prominent among the latter was a twenty-year-old with intense blue eyes, called Phoebe, whose consciousness had been raised to an inordinate height.

Heath-Morecomb, her feet up on the desk and looking unaccountably well, considering the late hours she kept, was taking her on.

Phoebe was stressing a point. "We have to make it clear that this is a *womanaction!* No more male domination! We don't take a backseat! We don't submit!"

Heath-Morecomb waved her down. "We can hardly hold seminars on female suppression while we're marching. We need ideas for graphics, cartoons, pictures, banners. On the issue, please. The issue being world catastrophe."

"No, we're angry, we're angry, we want to say something about women's rage!"

"Oh, to hell with women's rage, Phoebe, what difference will it make who dominates the ashes? Do get your priorities sorted out."

"Mine are all sorted! We're here because we're *women!* Because militarism and sexism are the same thing!"

"We're here because we're interested in survival. Everybody's. Men's, women's, horses', kangaroos'."

"Listen, it's *men* who are going to drop those bombs. It's *men* who have always trashed the world. It's *men* who want to keep us from having any say in whether we live or die. It's *men* we're fighting."

Heath-Morecomb leaned back with her hands clasped behind her head. "Balls, Phoebe," she said, languorously.

Next door I found the coffee pot, and Lotte making a list. Within minutes I'd been sent to town on a supply run: T-hinges, 20d nails, exterior grade half-inch plywood, caulking cartridge, peanut butter, bread loaves, hamburger meat, scratch pads, pencils, sterile gauze, aspirin, garden stakes, twine. . . .

The day passed. Late in the afternoon I came across Harriet and asked her about the meeting that morning. She said the official reaction to Dakin was that there was nothing to fear from that quarter. And with her small smile, added, "Which is exactly what we thought they'd say."

"Well, then—what's going to happen?"

She shook her head and went off on some errand, looking tired.

I had the early security shift that night, eight to twelve, and was entertained for the first part of it by a group that sat on the ground between two tents rehearsing a sort of folk song composed by the girl who was playing the guitar, an intensely serious person who weighed about ninety pounds, of which at least fifty belonged to a pigtail that hung down to her waist.

A little before eleven, with the camp dark and quiet, Brenda came seeking me out as I made my rounds.

"Hey! Fantastic! Listen to this: there's a rumor going around that Alice Dakin is gone!"

"What do you mean, *gone?*"

"*Gone,* you know, disappeared."

"You mean she packed up and left town?" Was that what the officials had meant by "nothing to fear from that quarter"?

"I don't know about 'packed up.' They didn't say."

"They who?"

"The people at the Sycamore. Michael said he went—"

"Michael?"

"The documentary! The moustache! He went up there to see if he could find out if any counterdemonstrators were in town and where, and the place was full of cops—well, two or three, and a patrol car, and the waitress in the dining room told him Dakin's people were hysterical, they couldn't find her anywhere."

"Her *people* are still here? That doesn't make sense."

"Don't knock it, she's gone. Wherever she went, better there than here."

We were crossing the dark, deserted back boundary, and Brenda began to look nervously over her shoulder. At a sudden noise from the woods she jumped, yelping. I swung my flashlight toward the edge of the woods. Nothing.

"Shit," she said, "this is some job you've got. I'd rather grow radishes." But, loyally, she stayed until I'd completed the round, making conversation.

"So where do you think she is? Dakin? Maybe she ran off with some Air Force general."

"My God, Brenda."

"Why not? Uniforms are sexy, right?"

"In a peace camp, that's treason you're talking."

"Yeah, but in life it's a fact. Even that guy who put the cuffs on us. Old, but sexy."

Old? He couldn't be any older than Elliot. And Elliot was barely older than I was.

"Anyway," she went on, caught up in her fantasy, "I think that's a great idea. She gets invited to some pro-Pentagon party, has a few too many scotches, this John Wayne type makes a pass—"

"At *Dakin?*"

"I *said* they were drunk. When he sobers up he'll kill himself. In the meantime he gets her into his jeep, or whatever those generals drive, and says 'Let's go to Honolulu,' because he's sentimental about Pearl Harbor."

"Not quite his branch of the service."

"Oh well, whatever."

"No. I know it's spring and all that, but I don't think Dakin is a woman for this season. If she's gone anywhere, it's to persuade the National Guard to come in and put us under tent arrest."

"If she went somewhere on business, her people would know where she was."

"There is that." Privately, I thought that either the documentary man had dreamed it up to get some shots of the women in a dither, or the waitress at the Sycamore had interpreted whatever was going on with a fine disregard for fact and a small-town flair for scandal. "We'll find out in the morning," I said, "the Brain Trust will know."

In the morning, however, no one knew anything, not even Doris, whose fingers, I felt sure, must be stiff from constantly taking the civic pulse.

Harriet asked me if I would pick up a batch of encampment handbooks from the printer in West Crannock, and I agreed. "Just tell me how to get there."

"Lotte will give you directions."

But I couldn't find Lotte anywhere, two other women I asked had never heard of West Crannock, and I decided not to waste time. I'd have to stop first at a gas station, in any case, to fill up the tank, and I could find out there. The gas station, on the wide main street in Padua, was busy; both sets of pumps were being used. I pulled up behind a white Chevy with a gum-chewing attendant running a squeegee over the windshield, and waited, idly watching the sparse activity along the street. On the far side a limp-looking man came out of Quality Cleaners, carrying a plastic-covered suit on a hanger. A short, dapper man went briskly into Boylan Real Estate and Insurance. A tall, dark-haired girl in a hurry began to cross the street. There was a sudden blast from the horn of the Chevy in front of me, and the woman behind the wheel got out of the car and called to the girl: "Lynette!"

I recognized the driver: the woman from the class reunion at the Sycamore, the one who'd called the camp a hotbed of terrorist troublemakers, the one I'd seen again in the Sycamore lobby before the Dakin conference, she of the uncreasable clothes. The girl ran the rest of the way across the street and up to the car, long legs flashing below the skirt, attracting a prolonged look from the gum-chewing young man who was detaching the hose from the back end of the Chevy.

"Hi, *Ethel!*" the girl squealed. "Oh thank you *so* much! They're so *pretty!*"

"They all arrived in good condition, I hope? No broken cups or saucers?"

"No, they're *beautiful.* We love them. Bruce thinks they're neat. What were you doing in *Schenectady?*"

"Schenectady? What makes you think I was in Schenectady?"

84

"There was a slip in the box, from the store in Schenectady."

The gumchewer handed "Ethel" the charge pack for her signature and I turned the key in the ignition, preparing to move up, but the woman stood there, holding the pack and the ballpoint, oblivious of the attendant waiting, indifferent to the fact that other vehicles needed to be serviced, lost in the earthshaking matter of the slip from the store.

"Oh, no," she said. "No, I guess Rand's has a store there too. You know how they do, when they run out of stock, get it sent from another branch. No, I ordered it at Rand's right here. How do you like the apartment?"

The gumchewer wandered off to take care of a pickup truck that had pulled into the space vacated by a car on the other side of the service island. I drummed my fingers impatiently on the steering wheel.

"Oh, those new apartments are really neat," the girl babbled on. "Not that I get to see much of it. Mom's taking care of everything, she waits for them to deliver things, fixes everything up, you know Mom and her superstitions; it's bad luck for the bride to fix up her own place before the wedding. We don't even get the key until we're *man and wife,* can you believe it? Anyway, I'm having a final fitting on the gown this morning. Three more days! I'm so nervous!"

I was pleased to see that "Ethel" had finally become aware of the charge pack in her hand and was signing it. Talking, though, all the while. "Nice that the base gave you an extra week off to get yourself ready."

"I would've *died* if they hadn't. Except I wish I had a car. Dad's always taking the car and staying away for hours. It'd be great if he went to work in the morning, like everybody else, so I could have the car during the day, but he doesn't even *ask* if I need it. He's really moody these days."

"Your dad's all right, it's just that all fathers *hate* for their daughters to get married."

My fingers hovered over the horn, itching to blow it at them. The sun was streaming in through the window, the car was heating up.

"Can I give you a lift somewhere?"

"Well, if you're going by Garrison Street. That's where my fitting is."

"Sure. I'll drop you off."

The girl ran around the car and scrambled into the passenger seat and the gumchewer came up and took the charge pack from the woman, and I poised my foot over the accelerator. But no.

"Wait!" she said, grabbed the pack from his hand, pulled out the charge sheets. "I'll pay cash for this."

I closed my eyes. This was my fate. If there were four checkout counters in a supermarket, I ended up in the one catering to a shopper cashing in four hundred coupons.

"Ethel" doled out some money and tore the charge sheets into several pieces. "Don always has a fit when he sees the gasoline bills," she said to her passenger.

I could just see this woman intimidated by a mere husband. It was as likely as a Wagnerian diva cowering at a cross word from a spear carrier.

Finally, *finally,* she got behind the wheel and drove off, and I moved up to the pump.

While the boy with the gum filled the tank, I went into the office for directions. The man gave me a map.

West Crannock proved to be a dismal little town fifteen miles to the east that could not be reached by any straightforward route, but had to be approached circuitously, by way of many implausible turnings and backtrackings, all designed to discourage any but the most resolute visitor. I turned on the car radio. Nothing but the screech and moan currently referred to by the populace as music. I turned it off. Ahead of me a yellow trailer bumped along at eleven miles an hour in the middle of the road, interminably, until it finally turned off at a sign saying TRAILER CAMP. It took almost an hour to get there, and when I finally found J. C. Griffith, Printing, Quick Copy Offset,

Forms and Billheads, a sour, hollow-chested man with cheeks full of broken blood vessels told me the handbooks had not yet been stapled together. Another long hour slid by as I waited for them, walking up and down the hot street that smelled of tar, enjoying West Crannock's sole cultural amenity, two pimpled youths polishing a ten-year-old Oldsmobile with a FOR SALE sign on it, parked, for some reason, in the middle of a front lawn.

By the time I got back to the camp, the morning was gone. I felt sweaty and frayed at the edges, longed to be home standing under the shower in my bathroom, with clean, unrumpled clothes hanging decently in the bedroom closet. On my way to the washhouse to settle for another sink-splash, I wondered, yet again, if what I was doing here was really going to keep the world from going over the edge, into the abyss.

I wondered, too, if and when there would be repercussions from the "message" left at the base. Would the MPs be searching for the perpetrators? Or would they pretend it never happened, to avoid publicity?

Brenda, in the wash-house scrubbing the agricultural grime from her hands and face, said she was starving, and why didn't we go to the Plaza for lunch.

"I've heard worse suggestions," I said. If not home, at least to the Plaza. "Let's go."

The sight of the flaking marquee and mullioned windows cheered me, and I followed Brenda from the bright sunlight into the dim interior feeling lighthearted. It was the last time I was to feel lighthearted for quite a while.

In the lobby, Brenda said, "I'm going to say hello to Julius," and disappeared into the bar.

It wasn't Julius she was looking for, of course. The spring plague was roiling around in Brenda's blood, and the object of it had a moustache. Not that he was likely to be here in the middle of a workday, but reason has no hold on the libido.

I turned into the dining room, with its red-clothed tables. Long and narrow, twin to the bar, with yet another

87

baroque chandelier hanging from its high ceiling, the tall window fronting on the street draped in dark red velveteen festooned with fringe, each table decorated with an imitation cut-crystal bud vase containing one perfect plastic rose. Like the rest of the hotel, it was at the same time elegant, tacky and endearing.

We were late for the lunch hour and the room was empty. Except for one table against the far wall. There was very definitely someone at that table. A plate of antipasto in front of him. An open book on the table beside the plate. Wispy gray hair catching a shaft of light from the window. Pale green chinos. Bottle-green and saffron-yellow checked sport shirt completely at odds with the long, furrowed face. Slouching like an elongated question mark, in a straight wooden chair designed for sitting bolt upright.

I'm hallucinating, I thought. *Dear God, I'm in a bad way. Did I forget to have breakfast? Have I not had enough sleep? Am I coming down with a bug?*

Greenfield? At the Plaza? In Padua?

CHAPTER EIGHT

GREENFIELD LOOKED UP FROM THE TABLE, SAW me and one caterpillar eyebrow rose in acknowledgment.

I crossed the room Ophelia-like, and he didn't vanish. It was Greenfield, all right. Well, well. The situation must be desperate if he actually drove all this way to argue me back to Poplar Avenue. Private universe falling apart without the main cog in his life-support system? I tried to keep the satisfaction from showing.

"*Charlie?*"

He regarded me with casual interest and inquired, "What are you doing here?"

"*Me?* What am *I* doing . . . ?"

"I don't mean the geographical area. I mean"—he indicated the room—"this Sherwood Anderson setting. Shouldn't you be out there parading with a sign?"

Well, if he wanted to descend to *that* level. "We're allowed twenty minutes for lunch."

He nodded as though he believed it and studied my appearance. "You look," he decided, "as though you've spent six nights in a Bulgarian cave in the aftermath of an earthquake."

I nodded back. I thought *he* looked as though he were going to ride in the Kentucky Derby, but I didn't say so. "Well, I *feel* fine," I said. "It's just that around here we don't live quite the way they do at the Cannes Film Festival."

I was about to sit down when his eyes went past me to the doorway and he rose, albeit unhurriedly, to his feet. I turned to look. Heath-Morecomb came across the room, dressed much as I was, but somehow looking as though she'd spent six nights in a scented hot tub listening to Brahms.

Well, of course!

Why else would he be here, stupid.

Something rose to my throat and stayed there.

Drove all the way up from Sloan's Ford just to have lunch with her. Called the camp and asked her to meet him. Didn't even tell me he was here. Stood up when she entered the room. Not just an eyebrow, stood up!

Heath-Morecomb opened her mouth to say something that was no doubt pithy and brilliant, but I forestalled her.

"I'd better get Brenda," I said urgently. "She's in the bar. I just remembered—we promised to do something—for—Harriet."

I started out of the room and collided with Brenda coming in.

"Let's go," I murmured.

"*What? Why?*"

"It's too late. They're out of food."

"They can't be. Julius just told me to order the veal."

She moved past me, saw Heath-Morecomb, called out to her, sat down at a table and picked up a menu.

Impossible situation.

I leaned over the table. "Brenda," I said quietly, "I'm feeling a little queasy. I think the sight of food would be dangerous. I'll wait for you in the bar." And while she gaped, I left.

At the bar, I drank ginger ale and sat watching Julius rubbing down the beautiful counter with lemon oil as he carried on an idle argument with a tired-looking man in shirt sleeves who had draped his suit jacket over one of the stools.

Bulgarian cave. Did I really look that bad? I hadn't thought about it. I hadn't been paying that much attention. A splash of water, a quick brush through my hair. I wasn't here to model clothes. Neatness doesn't count when you're trespassing. The ginger ale tasted bitter. I raised my eyes and looked at my image in the enormous mirror behind the bar. Pretty bad. Not the best thing for self-esteem, which is battered enough as it is. I must clean myself up, wash my hair, something.

"Julius," I said, during a pause in the argument, "does this hotel have guest rooms?"

"Twenty," he said proudly, black-grape eyes shining.

"Showers?"

"Not all of them," he admitted. "You have a friend coming up? I don't have one with a shower for tonight. The latest check-in took the last one. Unless he would change for a room with a bath. I'll ask him, if you want; he's in the dining room."

"No, never mind."

Trust Greenfield to get the last shower. How did he *find* this place, anyway? Coming into town along the main arteries, you couldn't possibly run across it accidentally. Unless, of course, *she* had told him about it. What else had she told him? What was she telling him at this moment?

I thought about bathtubs as opposed to showers. I hated sitting in cooling water full of soiled soapsuds. It wasn't much better than staying unwashed. Maybe I'd adjust to my new image: Maggie Rome, cave-woman.

But I knew I wouldn't. For me, at the moment, a state of depression would have been an improvement.

Somehow I made the ginger ale last until Brenda was ready to leave, and we went out to where the car was parked in the small weedy lot next to the hotel. The only other vehicle present was a worn-out red panel truck. Where, now that I thought about it, was Greenfield's Plymouth? I unlocked the passenger door for Brenda to get in and went around to the driver's side.

"Maggie."

There was only one voice that could command across a hundred feet of parking lot without being raised by so much as a decibel. I glanced over my shoulder. Greenfield was coming toward me at his leisurely pace. What now? I went, cautiously, to meet him, and we stopped a few feet apart, trading inscrutable looks.

"If it's within the realm of possibility," he said, "that you'll have a free hour or two sometime today, I want to talk to you."

"About what?"

He gave me a long look and a touch of the old stiletto. "I thought we might discuss the relative merits of the horses scheduled to run at Saratoga."

"You have company."

"That's not a permanent state of affairs."

"Anyway, I can't talk in my condition. I'm too dirty. If I find someplace where I can take a shower, I'll let you know when I'm free."

"A shower comes with the room I've booked."

"Well, I should hope so. You wouldn't want to walk around looking as though you'd spent the night in a cave."

One corner of his mouth twitched upward. "Reprisal," he said, reaching into a pocket, "is not the most inventive form of discourse." He handed me a large key with a wooden number tag. "The company should be gone within the hour"—and he walked away.

Brenda, who'd seen the encounter but not heard the

exchange, was virtually vibrating with astonishment as I got behind the wheel.

"Jesus!" she said. "What's going on? He has lunch with H.-M. and he gives you the key to his room? What is it, some kind of kinky party?"

I rested my head against the wheel and laughed uncontrollably.

"Well, come on." Brenda was indignant. "I mean, who would have thought a person like *you*—"

"He's my boss," I managed. "I'm only going to take a shower."

Apparently she took this to be such a flagrant lie that she pointedly dropped the subject and spent the ride back to the camp describing the culinary delights I'd missed by settling for ginger ale. I was beginning to regret it myself: appetite was returning. I was in a measurably better frame of mind. In those few words with Greenfield, I felt some barrier between us had been dissolved. Probably I'd been making too much of his contact with Heath-Morecomb. There was nothing to say, for instance, that they hadn't met here by accident, as he and I had. And "I want to talk to you"? What could that mean, except what my instinct had first told me: he'd come here to argue me back home to the *Reporter.* Not that I'd go, but since when was that as important as being asked?

At the camp, I hurried to the tent, grabbed a few clean, if rumpled, clothes and went back to the car, watched, slit-eyed, by a clearly speculating Brenda, who then went off to paint slogans on balloons for the demonstration march. Her fantasy about Alice Dakin would be milk and water compared with the one she was clearly dreaming up about me. Why explain? Why spoil her fun? Glowing in anticipation of a downpour of hot water, I headed back toward the road.

And a white patrol car with two men in the front seat turned off the road into the track and came toward me.

Police? Oh, God. They'd found the one piece of barbed wire I'd clipped and they were after me.

93

I pulled onto the field grass to let them by, but they stopped short of me. Not *now*, I thought crazily, not before I've had my shower! Then I saw that it wasn't the Air Force patrol car. No stripes on the side. No star, either, so it wasn't the sheriff's department. Must be the city police.

So it wasn't a fence clipper they were tracking down.

Padua, though it strained belief, was legally a city, and fine jurisdictional lines determined which kind of justice prevailed: at the base, up to a certain number of feet past the fence, it was military; beyond that the sheriff's department took over, or the city police, depending on whether or not county roads were involved, or some such. At the camp there might be reason for a sheriff's car to come calling, but the city police?

The man in the passenger seat got out of the car, came up to my window. Plain clothes. A detective? The FBI?

"You staying at this camp?" A notebook the size of a paperback looked lost in his big left hand.

I said yes, I was staying at the camp.

"Name, please?"

I gave him my name, wondering if I really had to, wishing I had Doris there to advise me. "What's this all about?"

"We're investigating a police matter."

"What kind of police matter?"

He looked at me with eyes the color and warmth of slate. "We're just asking for your cooperation. Can you tell me where you were last Tuesday night?"

Tuesday night. I felt myself go rigid. Yes, of course, I remember it well. I was jumping over a barbed-wire fence onto the Air Force grounds. "What time Tuesday night?"

He registered the implication of that question, but didn't pursue it. "From ten P.M. on."

My muscles relaxed. "I was at the bar in the Plaza hotel. With a friend from the camp. In the presence of five other people. Until eleven-thirty or so. Then I was back here at the camp, on security patrol."

As I said it I suddenly recalled *"Go where people will see you and remember you."*

He took something from a pocket. "You ever see this before?"

It was a wide white hatband with black lettering. BAND, it said, just as it had when it was wrapped around Heath-Morecomb's straw boater.

I looked at it, and my muscles contracted again. Where had he found it? On the runway at the base? No, that would be a matter for the MPs. Where, then? And why had he brought it here? What made him think it belonged to someone at the camp?

One thing was certain: he wasn't returning it as a courtesy.

I shook my head. "No," I said. "Never saw it before."

He continued looking at me for a while, then put the band back in his pocket, nodded briefly, went back to the patrol car, and the car continued up the track toward the barn.

I hesitated, but only fractionally, and took off. Whatever was going on could not possibly be as urgent as a shower. At the hotel I ignored the dining room and scooted up the stairs.

The second floor of the Plaza had clearly been conceived in a spirit more dedicated to the functional than the ornamental; even so, the ceiling was high, the hallway moldings boasted a raised pattern of vine leaves, and the doors to the rooms were wide and deeply paneled. Holding Greenfield's large room key with its wooden number tag, I walked to the end of the hallway, inserted the key in the lock of room number nine, and opened the door.

A corner room, three tall windows with rose-colored drapes overlooking the street, twin beds with vintage headboards, one plump armchair in a flowered print, Greenfield's suitcase on a luggage rack, an open door in one wall revealing a piece of tile floor beyond, and a section of curtained, claw-footed bathtub. Good enough.

I put my clean T-shirt, jeans and underwear on the

tufted bedspread and tore off what I was wearing. Tamped down at the back of my mind, the nagging question of what Heath-Morecomb's hatband was doing in the hands of a city detective awaited a more propitious moment. When I was clean and at peace, when I'd had my little "talk" with Greenfield, I would go back to the camp and find out what was going on. Right now I didn't want to think about it. I had climbed up to a state of depression and even out of it: Greenfield showed some signs of returning to sanity, he even recognized my existence, I was going to have a shower, things were looking up. I padded, barefoot and naked, into the bathroom.

The bathroom was scented.

Delicately but unmistakably.

With the scent of lavender.

I traced it to a small, empty, feminine, British bottle in the waste basket.

I sat down on the edge of the tub.

When? For how long? How many times had she been in this room? *How long had Greenfield been in Padua?*

I suddenly remembered Heath-Morecomb's strange nocturnal wandering at 3:00 A.M. the night of my first security patrol, her odd, excited, feverish look. I'd put it down to the nervous business of having carted that stuff onto the base. But she'd had ample time to recover from that, she and the others would have been back at the camp for four hours by then. *If* she'd come back with them. *If* she hadn't merely dropped them off and driven on to the Plaza.

But that was Tuesday night. It was unthinkable that Greenfield would have left his office on a Tuesday, the day before the *Reporter* went to press. He couldn't possibly. He wouldn't. *Would he? Was it that bad?*

I closed my eyes. Elliot was right after all. It was jealousy. Abject, disgusting, insufferable jealousy. Because Heath-Morecomb, let's face it, was not another Madame X, whose existence didn't bother me, who, from all I'd sensed, merely cooked, listened, shared her bed with him from time to time, and generally waited around for his occasional visits, another Madame Maigret, a sort of wife-without-portfolio. Madame X was fine with me. She inhabited another plane. She didn't encroach on my territory. She was not his *companion*. It was not her function to amuse him, anger him, engage his wit. That was *my* exclusive province.

That *had* been my exclusive province.

Now, apparently, a lavender-scented Brit had marched in and taken not just one province, but the whole damn country.

If there'd been room for doubt before, the bottle in the waste basket had taken care of that.

I swallowed, with difficulty. What was I swallowing? Anger? Pride? Medicine?

I climbed into the bathtub, tucked the shower curtain inside it, and washed, washed, washed.

Finally, clean, dry, and smelling of nothing but soap and shampoo, I dressed, picked up my pile of discarded clothes and went downstairs. Greenfield was in the bar, sitting at a table with Julius, a triple A road map spread out between them.

"Sure," Julius was saying, "it's not a superhighway, but it cuts off this whole triangle here and takes you right to the Thruway, and that gets you onto the Mass. Turnpike and you cut straight across to 495. Get you there by early afternoon." He looked up, saw me standing there with Greenfield's room key dangling from my fingers, grinned, and tactfully withdrew to his post behind the magnificent mahogany bar. After this, I thought, dimly, Brenda wouldn't be the only one speculating on the activities in room number nine.

Greenfield folded the map. "I'm going to Marlboro in the morning to spend a week or so. It's too early for the concerts, but Shura's son Vladi will be there. He's written a flute quartet and one of the groups is going to perform it. I can wander around the campus and catch a little of the rehearsals."

I gaped at him. Marlboro didn't surprise me: Greenfield had never voluntarily deserted his stereo for any place that didn't boast live music. But a *week or so* away from the *Reporter*, on impulse? Vacations were something he endured each July only because his staff demanded them and there was no way to put out a newspaper without staff.

"Who's minding the store?" I asked.

"The store," he said, "is on vacation."

"In *June?*" He had never left his office until July. Never.

"There comes a time"—he leaned back in the chair—"when consistency runs a poor second to hedonism."

Indeed. And five will get you ten that English Lavender is planning a few days off after the demonstration. In Marlboro.

I handed him the room key and looked away. I knew it was unreasonable to feel betrayed. Unintelligent, unbecoming, pointless, and I couldn't have felt otherwise if the consequence were death by walking the plank.

"Thanks for the shower," I mumbled. "What do you want to talk about?"

He studied my face, lynx-eyed under the bushy eyebrows. "Was the water tepid?"

"No, it was fine. Why?"

He picked up the map. "I've heard more enthusiasm," he said, "from a ten-year-old boy unwrapping a birthday gift and finding six handkerchiefs." He got to his feet. "Too many distractions here to talk easily." At a leisurely pace he led me out of the bar, back up the stairs, down the hallway and into the room.

I'd had enough of that room. I stood by the door.

"What is it, Charlie? It's late, I have to get back."

"You seem to be going at a killing pace these days. Perhaps you'd better give up the business of *making* news, and go back to merely *covering* it." He picked up a folded newspaper from the dresser top and brought it to me.

It was the Padua *Ledger*. A heading glared up from the page: FIVE PROTESTERS ENTER AIR FORCE BASE. And below that: *A spokeswoman for the Women's Peace Camp stated yesterday that on Tuesday night, five women from the encampment successfully made their way onto Hunegger Air Force base grounds and taped a two-hundred-foot strip of canvas across the end of the runway. The message painted on the canvas in letters five feet high said, "The End of the World Begins Here." The five women left the base without being apprehended.*

The article went on to say the base authorities acknowledged finding the message, but had no comment on the incident. The rest was filler, a rehash of basic information about the camp, previous incidents that had taken place, and reactions of local officials. Names of the "five protesters" had, of course, not been volunteered by the anonymous spokeswoman.

Well, I thought, she's done it. Got herself a headline.

I crossed to the dresser, handed him the paper, went back to the door, shifted my bundle of clothes from one hand to the other, and made no comment.

"Maggie, you're unsettling me. You look as though you're about to run for the border. Light . . . somewhere."

I sat, gingerly, on the edge of the bed. "What do you want to talk about, Charlie?"

He leaned back against the dresser. "For one thing," he said, taking his time, "Elliot is somewhere west of the Mississippi. If there's a chance he's going to return to find that I went off to Marlboro leaving you to be incarcerated, I want to know about it in time to move my belongings to another continent."

Oh, that. "Not me," I said.

"Could you spare a whole sentence?"

"I wasn't one of the five, if that's what you're asking. Besides, I'm not your responsibility, or anyone else's. I'm a grown woman. I'm so grown I'm beginning to hate it. Besides that, even if I *had* been one of the five, the authorities have no way of knowing who those five people are. And besides that, they didn't damage government property, and trespassing in itself isn't necessarily a cause for incarceration."

He looked down at the newspaper in his hand, turned it over. "I'm relieved to hear it. There's a companion piece"—and handed it to me again, right-hand side of the page facing up.

A box. Center, outlined.

PRO-NUCLEAR-FORCE LECTURER DISAPPEARS *According to staff members, Alice Dakin, well-known author of* Why God Gave Us the Bomb, *who was staying at the Sycamore Inn in Padua, failed to return from a small private dinner party on the grounds of Hunegger Air Force Base on Tuesday night. Edward Beck, Mrs. Dakin's secretary, said that Mrs. Dakin was last seen at about ten-thirty Tuesday night as she got into her car to leave the base. Police are combing . . .* I dropped the paper on the bed, stunned. *Ten-thirty. Tuesday night. At the base.*

"Quite a bonanza for the Padua *Ledger,*" Greenfield said. "All they had to do was print those two items side by side. Hearst couldn't have done better."

I heard him with half my mind. The other half was taking off in all directions, like a pile of assorted firecrackers ignited by a tossed match. Had they known she was going to be on the base at that time? Planned the runway business as a cover? Or saw her there and gave in to spur-of-the-moment insanity? What had they done with her? Was that why—?

Police are combing . . .

"I have to make a call." I found myself going down the stairs to the bar.

"Julius, is there a public phone around here?"

"If you want to make a local call"—he beamed—"you can use this one." He brought a telephone from under the bar, put it on the newly polished wood, and I dialed the number of the camp. Doris picked it up on the first ring, sounding, if possible, even grimmer than usual.

Julius had gone to the far end of the bar to talk with his single patron, and the drone from the talking head on the television screen spread a miasma of sound over the immediate vicinity, but I moved away for good measure, as far as the cord would let me. "Doris, it's Maggie. A patrol car pulled into the camp as I was leaving, about an hour ago, and one of the cops asked me a few questions. What was that all about?"

Doris thought carefully before replying: she was convinced the camp phones were tapped. "Alice Dakin," she said, "is missing."

"I know that. Why did they come to the camp?"

"They just found Dakin's car on a back road near Hunegger Mills."

"And?"

"And they're trying to pin it on us, what else?"

"Why were they asking about—" Who knows, the line *might* be tapped. "—about some hatband? What does that have to do with it?"

There was a pause. I could almost see her pushing up the bridge of her glasses with one finger, wondering if I'd told the cops I recognized it.

"They claim," she said, "they found the hatband on the floor of Dakin's car."

CHAPTER NINE

I WENT SLOWLY BACK UP THE STAIRS, TRYING TO think coherently about the repercussions of this crazy, irresponsible act of Heath-Morecomb and company. God, that woman with her bloody theatrics, her penchant for riding roughshod over everyone, her British version of *L'état, c'est moi!* Damn it, I'd come up here, gone through all that business of stalking around in the dark, all that tension, all that fear, because it was important to protest, it was important not to sit home and just watch the bombs pile up. And now they'd turned it all into a shambles. Jeopardized our credibility, the demonstration, the camp, thrown mud on the whole antinuclear movement. How could they have *done* it!

Well, they had. And now what? Was the damage irreversible? Or could something still be salvaged?

I stopped at the top of the stairs and stared at the motif of vine leaves on the hallway moldings. It wasn't the first time I'd stumbled on a crime and found myself, for one reason or another, trying to unravel it. Abduction, this time. Let's *hope* abduction, and not worse. The others had all been worse. This, though, could escalate into a real horror. Dakin followers descending on Hunegger Mills. Reprisals against the camp. Confrontation . . .

If only Dakin would walk back into the Sycamore on her own two snippy little feet and announce that she'd had a bout of amnesia.

If only someone would find her somewhere, drunk as a coot.

If only she'd *reappear*.

But of course she couldn't.

If only I knew where they'd *put* her.

Would that defuse the situation, to find her? Have her "rescued" by a contingent from the peace camp? Could it be done? Of course it could. All it needed was a troop of Girl Scouts. And a helicopter. And maybe the Marines.

And someone to figure out where to start looking.

I looked down the hallway to room number nine. Behind that door was the man who, in previous crimes of my acquaintance, had done all the unraveling. But he was leaving in the morning.

I went on down the hallway, knocked on the door and went in. Greenfield was occupying the fat, flower-printed armchair by the windows, the ankle of one long leg resting on the knee of the other, marking out his route on the road map with a yellow Hi-Liner. I sat down on the edge of the bed and watched him, silently, until he looked up, examining my face for a clue to what was going on. "Whatever's on your mind," he said, "you're clearly not enjoying it."

"I'm trying to figure out how to bring back Alice Dakin."

He put the map on the bed and the Hi-Liner on top of it. "I've known you to have some peculiar yearnings before this, Maggie, but a nostalgia for an infectious virus somehow verges on the eccentric."

"It's a trade-off. The sooner she's found, the less chance of the camp going down the drain. I know you don't think these protests are going to make an iota of difference, but as far as I can see they're the only game in town, and for whatever good they can do, I'd hate to find them banned by law."

"There *is* a First Amendment."

"Today. No guarantee about tomorrow. We do, after all, have the fastest reinterpreter in the West keeping an eye on things. One abduction of a bigot by a group of protesters and you'll hardly recognize the Bill of Rights."

"Your interpretation of the workings of a democracy is fascinating."

"There's nothing wrong with my understanding of how a pendulum swings."

"Maggie. Five protesters and one bigot happened to pass in the night. That's hardly grounds for the abolition of free speech."

"There's a little more to it, Charlie. It won't surprise me, for instance, if the British embassy is shortly informed that one of Her Majesty's subjects has committed a serious crime on foreign soil."

I watched his face, expecting to see shock. If not shock, maybe pain. If neither of those, at least anxiety. What I saw was the dean of the English department faced with a faculty member who has just uttered a solecism.

"Remarkable," he said dryly, to the suede loafer on his left foot, "there are professional detectives the world over who have spent decades of their lives in the pursuit of criminals, and still have files full of crimes that remain unsolved. But you, after only a few amateur experiences in the field, can make one phone call and unerringly identify a perpetrator."

He refused to believe it!

"You were quick enough to identify *me*, with all that talk about Elliot and incarceration and whatnot."

"I merely thought it was a possibility you'd walked on their grass without permission, a crime the military handbook is quite capable of classifying as cause for prosecution. That's a far cry from convicting someone of abduction."

"You don't know what's been going on at the camp!"

"If you're saying she was one of the five women who were at the base that night, I assume you have good reason for saying it. Anything beyond that—barring a signed confession—is pure extrapolation. You read the *Ledger* and fell right into the trap." He got out of the chair, moved to the window and stood looking down at the street, a hard case of relentless self-deception.

"Charlie, could you, just once, accept the possibility that I might know a few things you don't know?"

"I never question your knowledge, only your wisdom."

Oh-ho! And what a vast acreage that word *wisdom* could cover!

"Right." I picked up my parcel of clothes and started for the door. "Enjoy yourself in Marlboro."

"Don't dissemble, Maggie," he said to the window. "You didn't come in here and announce you were planning a search for a missing bigot merely to pass the time of day. That revelation was designed to *keep* me from Marlboro."

"*Keep* you!" The only thing Greenfield had ever successfully been kept from was playing a B flat, and that was on being confronted by a score clearly marked B natural. It took *Beethoven* to keep him from something.

He turned away from the window. "Let's have it. Whatever it is you know. The whole staggering body of incontrovertible fact." He waited, in a state of resolute skepticism, dead certain I had nothing to offer but an overheated imagination.

I dropped my parcel back on the bed. "I can't give it to you out of context, you have to know something about these people."

"I'm listening."

Listening, yes. Hearing? I could only hope. I kicked off my flats and sat cross-legged on the bedspread.

"First of all," I said, "whatever you think, the camp is not just a collection of emotionally overwrought females. For the most part these women are intelligent, well informed, well organized and ingenious. And timidity is not one of their salient characteristics, especially when it comes to confronting the proponents of nuclear weapons. In fact, to describe them in that regard, I'd have to revise the definition of 'inexorable' upward."

"Don't bother, the message comes across."

"As for Alice Dakin, obviously she's a threat at any time, but right now she poses an *immediate* danger. The camp is going to be the base for a major demonstration this weekend, and Dakin came here for the specific purpose of disrupting it."

"It would hardly take a political analyst to deduce that."

I sighed, and struggled on. "The four people who really run things, aside from the British violinist we happen to know, are the camp organizers. They've all worked in some national or international organization: the Peace Alliance, the Women's Action for Peace and Justice, the International League for Peace. So they're not naïve, they've been around the block a couple of times, and they're not just dedicated, they're *consecrated.*" I told him about the individual and collective reactions of JoAnne, Harriet, Doris, Lotte and Heath-Morecomb to the news that Alice Dakin had arrived to stage a counterdemonstration. About my being sent to "cover" the Dakin publicity business. About Heath-Morecomb's scheme for entering the base Tuesday night, and the part Brenda and I played in it.

He listened, nodding in a remote sort of way, about as vitally involved as if I were describing some bank holdup in Indonesia.

"Well," I said, all but drawing diagrams, "it was *those five consecrated women*—who went onto the base Tuesday night—about ten P.M. And it was thirty minutes later that Dakin was seen—on that *same* base—for the last time."

He took his hands out of his pockets and folded his arms across his chest. "And those five women, being, as you said, intelligent, well informed and well organized, disposed of Mrs. Dakin and immediately thereafter called the local newspaper and placed themselves indisputably at the scene of the crime."

"Come on, Charlie, you know why they did that. They knew the camp would be suspect and they deflected suspicion in advance. What better way to prove their innocence? Who'd believe a guilty group in its right mind would voluntarily admit to being at the relevant place at the crucial time?"

"They thought that would deflect the police, did they? It wouldn't occur to these intelligent, well-informed women who've been around the block, as you say, that even in the hinterlands the police might have a passing acquaintance with deviousness?"

"It wouldn't occur to *me*."

The eyebrows went up, to indicate he would refrain from comment. "But it did occur to you that Dakin's disappearance would cause trouble for the camp. Apparently they overlooked that as well."

"It was a calculated risk. They probably reasoned that without proof it would die down."

"And what are they intending to do with Dakin once the demonstration is over? Kill her? Or release her so that she can go straight to the police and point her finger at them?"

"Any five-year-old box-watcher knows how you get around that. Stocking masks, painters' overalls, no talking: no identification. Anyway, Charlie, there's more." I got off the bed, went to the window and stood next to him, so that I wouldn't miss the slightest change of expression. "Heath-Morecomb wears a straw boater with a white band that has the word BAND lettered on it in big black letters. This morning the police found the car Dakin was

107

driving. That hatband was lying on the floor of the car."

He didn't flinch. He didn't grow pale. He didn't even blink. He just stared at me for a moment, then turned back to the window and stood there gazing across the street at the low roof of a resigned little neighborhood grocery that backed onto a disused railway line.

Finally he said, "A hatband that flaunts the word BAND doesn't sound like something she would wear."

"We all have our little flaws."

He shot me a quizzical glance, and began to wander around the room. "What makes you think it was hers?"

"It's not the kind of item you're likely to find by the gross around here. It's unique. Ask anybody. She's been wearing that hat all over the place."

"Was she wearing it Tuesday night when the five of them entered the base?"

"I wasn't there when they entered the base. She wasn't wearing it when we checked on the ladder, but when Brenda and I left, she was on her way back to the camp to collect the rest of the crew and the canvas, so—"

"So presumably she collected the hat as well, wanting to be properly dressed for vaulting a barbed-wire fence, in her stocking mask and overalls."

"Charlie. It was *found*. In the *car*. A hatband doesn't travel under its own steam. It has to be transported from hither to yon by the person who's *wearing* it."

"Whoever," he pointed out, "that person might be."

I sagged. What was that again about the Emperor's Clothes?

"Someone"—he picked up the water decanter on the dresser and put it down again—"could have borrowed the hat."

"You don't borrow the royal crown."

"Or stolen it."

"She was wearing it Tuesday afternoon. She didn't leave the camp from then until the time we took her to where the ladder was. There was no breach of security at the camp that day or night, and there's been none since.

108

None of the campers would *dare* take it. And anyway, if she'd found her hat was missing, her outrage would have been audible in Nova Scotia."

"*If* the hat was missing."

"*If?*"

"We don't know it's the hat that's missing. All they found was the band. And that could have come loose and dropped off anywhere in her wanderings."

My God! "It came loose and dropped off in Dakin's *car,* is where it came loose and dropped off!"

His face remained calm, and unswervingly perverse.

I sank into the armchair, resigned to failure. This was FAITH. A man with FAITH beats a woman with LOGIC every time.

His mind could be changed, of course, by the simple expedient of having him ask her if she'd done it. But he wouldn't insult her by asking, because he *knew* she hadn't. And *I* certainly couldn't ask her: she was as likely to tell me the truth as she was to enter a nunnery. The same held true for the other four. No one outside the cabal would ever be privy to that secret. Certainly not me. I had miles to go before my *persona* became *grata* in that camp.

From my chair of pain, I asked, "Do you have an aspirin in that suitcase?"

He opened the suitcase, rummaged among the shirts and socks and books, finally found a small bottle under a copy of Vidal's *Lincoln,* and shook a couple of tablets into my hand. I filled a glass at the bathroom tap and swallowed the aspirin, knowing it wouldn't help. When I came back into the room, he was back at the window, looking out. There must be more to that view than was apparent to my eye.

I picked up my parcel of clothes. "I'd better be going."

He turned and crossed the room. "I'd be grateful if you'd drop me off at the garage that's tinkering with my car." He opened the door and we went into the hallway.

"The Plymouth?" I asked through a headache haze. "What's wrong with it?"

109

"It was making a noise." We went down the stairs. "The mechanic assured me it would take no more than a few hours to correct. I assume that means it was a five-minute job."

"Five minutes," I said, as we left the hotel and walked around to the small parking lot at the side, "only five minutes to track down the trouble and take care of it. Too bad he only works on cars."

I unlocked the passenger door of the Honda. Greenfield took his dashing new sunglasses from a pocket. "No amount of expertise would help you, Maggie. Not even a mechanic can find the source of a problem"—he put on the glasses—"unless you first define the problem accurately."

I confined my response to a heavy sigh, got in and started the car.

It would have been simple enough to drive up the narrow street on which the Plaza stood and make one straightforward turn onto the wide avenue that bisected the town—if my mind had been on getting to the avenue. But my mind was on Marlboro, on Heath-Morecomb, on Dakin, on my own dejection, on possibly cutting loose and going home, on what might be going on at the camp. . . .

"It seems to me," Greenfield said, "that the place I'm looking for must be somewhere in the other direction."

Oh, hell. Too late now, I'd have to go the long way around. "I know," I said without shame, "but this is a better route."

I took what I thought was a shortcut, and wound up on the road that went by the main entrance to the base. Damn.

"The route seemed remarkably shorter," Greenfield murmured, "when the cab took me from the garage to the hotel."

A mile farther on, I saw the grim line of large vehicles at the moment that Greenfield leaned forward, peering through the windshield. Up ahead, a convoy of trucks carrying what looked like military police was moving past the main gate.

"The town is apparently about to be occupied," he said, "or liberated, depending on your particular prejudice."

"Extra troops." I felt a chill in the region of my spine. "She *said* they were going to bring them in."

"What 'she' is it who said that?"

"Some woman. I overheard her talking to a friend. She seemed to have inside information that the base planned to augment the security force, because of the demonstration. Actually, she stopped just short of rubbing her hands in glee as she said it."

"That's the main entrance to the base?"

"That's it." I stopped at the curb, some yards before reaching the gate. The trucks went on down the road, presumably to some entrance closer to the barracks.

Quite a turnout at the gate. I spotted Brenda playing to the video boys' camera with a life-size cutout of a child looking up at a falling missile. An unprecedented percentage of the camp women were present, and a lot of women I'd never seen before, including a large young mother with an earthy, Scandinavian, Ingmar Bergman look, a baby resting against her ample bosom, tiny legs sticking out of a canvas sling hanging from the woman's neck. The demonstrators were beginning to arrive for the weekend.

The local citizens, too, were well represented. An unusual number of them were ranged along the curb facing the women. Drawn by the convoy of troops, or by the disappearance of Dakin and the possibility of trouble, or maybe just *Let's stop by on our way home from work and give 'em hell.* A few of them held signs:

WE PROTEST THE PROTESTERS
THIS IS OUR TOWN GO DEMONSTRATE IN YOUR OWN
WE WANT PEACE TOO, GET OUT AND LET US HAVE
SOME

Nothing about Dakin yet; possibly they hadn't had time to read the paper. But the faces were hostile, and there was shouting. One barrel-chested fortyish man in jeans, T-shirt and a baseball cap waved an American flag defiantly.

What country, I wondered, does he think *we're* trying to protect?

Greenfield was scrutinizing the scene with that bland, equivocal look that meant it would be etched on his inner eye for years to come. "Interesting," he said.

Glumly I muttered, "It's a civil war."

He grimaced. "An epic contradiction in terms if ever there was one."

I drove on, past the hostile people of the town, the man with the flag, Brenda with her arms raised and wrists crossed, chanting something. Her documentary hero was pointing his camera at the townsfolk as we drove by, and I thought how convenient it would be if there was a taped record of me driving my car past the base in case the Air Force ever wanted to prosecute me for lying.

At the next cross street I turned, found my way back to Padua's wide avenue and down through its neat, clean, joyless landscape.

The garage investigating the noise in Greenfield's Plymouth proved to be attached to the gas station where only that morning I'd waited to get the tank filled while the giver-of-china and the bride-to-be indulged in a mutual exchange of banalities. Now, of course, the pumps were idle. I pulled up to the open roll-up doors and Greenfield went in search of his mechanic. I waited to find out if the Plymouth was ready to leave, tried my car radio again. A dial full of commercials. Personal loans. Edie's Maternity Shop. Free landscaping estimates. The tail end of a newscast, a recall of some product, Hondas probably. The Jean Joint. Burke's Roofing. I clicked it off.

As Greenfield emerged from the dark recesses of the

garage, the gum-chewing attendant of the morning came out of the office and strolled in my direction.

"Hi," he called, remembering either the car or me. "Got a problem?"

I shook my head. My problem, defined or not, was beyond his help.

"That lady sure gave you a hard time this morning."

"It happens," I said, as Greenfield reached the car, and the gumchewer nodded and sauntered over to the pumps, where a car had drawn up.

Greenfield opened the passenger door and folded himself into the seat, leaving the door open. "You had a bad time this morning?"

"One of the town's less lovable people."

"What did you expect? In a town dependent for its livelihood on a military base, a peace camp sympathizer is about as likely as a Protestant member of the I.R.A."

"Nothing to do with that. Just forced to wait forever to get to the pump, because the woman ahead of me was having a chat with a passing acquaintance, instead of paying her bill and moving on. The same woman, by the way, who had the inside information about the extra troops at the base." All the day's misery and frustration now focused on "Ethel," in her plastic clothes. "Just stood there gabbing, ignoring the line of cars backed up and waiting. She's one of those people who would be very surprised to learn there are actual humans on this planet other than herself and a few personal friends. The rest of these things that walk and talk and drive cars belong to another species." I released the parking brake, fiercely. "If this were sixteenth-century Venice and Shylock cut himself and bled all over her shoes, she still wouldn't believe that red stuff came from his veins." I glared at the windshield. "Is the Plymouth ready?"

"It's ready."

"Good. Well then—I'll see you back in Sloan's Ford. Eventually."

He looked at me with a kind of impatient, tourist sympathy, a man passing quickly through problem country on his way to Elysium. "It's possible the reason for your headache is the lack of a proper meal in the recent past. Eat something: as an outlet, food is preferable to character assassination." He climbed out of the car and stood watching as the mechanic eased the Plymouth out of the darkness and into the light.

Desolate, I drove away.

CHAPTER TEN

TEN MINUTES LATER, FINDING MYSELF APPROACH-
ing the campground, I drove on by. I wasn't ready to face
all that. I had to think. About Dakin. And whether I was
really going to be stupid enough to try to find her, on my
own. A patently impossible task. She could be anywhere.

Well, not *any*where. Wherever they'd taken her, they'd
have to be able to keep an eye on her. And none of them
knew the area well enough to be familiar with likely hiding
places, except in the vicinity of the camp and the base. It
would have to be somewhere close to home. Particularly
so as they had to feed her. They couldn't risk long trips
three times a day. Somewhere close by . . .

I drove slowly around the perimeter of the base, scanning the adjacent ground: brush, trees, field grass, the
occasional house, clearly occupied. I drove on, past the

row of houses where Brenda and I had borrowed the ladder: the ladder was there, lying on the ground, the painting on that side finished. More open fields. Now a slight roll here and there in the contour of the land, not something you'd actually call a *hill,* but a small rise boasting only a covering of low vegetation. Another house, in the middle of nowhere, the half-acre around it cultivated. More field. And another house, and another. Nothing now for a couple of miles but brush and trees and roadside wildflowers. Another rise, with an old barn at the crest, against the horizon . . .

A barn.

I slowed, stopped, crept a few yards up a dirt track that led up the rise, shut off the engine, and sat there looking at the scene. A sizable, somewhat dilapidated gray barn, with a silo attached, just standing there, alone, at the top of the rise. No sign of a farmhouse anywhere. No sign of life. No field of corn or beans, or whatever else they grew around here. Abandoned, most likely, like the defunct factories around here. Another monument to a failing economy, to the changing times, to young people going off to more technological pastures.

What more suitable place for stowing a prisoner? Isolated, conveniently close to camp, a normal, innocent-looking part of the local landscape . . .

I could be up the track and into the barn in no time. But what if one of the Five showed up while I was in there? What if a cop, driving by, saw the strange Honda parked next to what he knew was an abandoned barn, and came to investigate?

No, Officer, I did not tie her up and leave her sitting in that silo, I didn't even know she was here, I just have this passion for looking around old barns. . . .

Of course, there was probably a place to park *behind* the barn, out of sight of the road. After all, one of the Five had to get here by car, to bring food and drink. On the other hand, out of sight of the road might be *in* sight of something else. A house on a distant rise of land, say.

Only one way to find out.

I drove up the rise and around to the back. An area of dry, pebbled dirt separated the barn from a stretch of sparse rough grass that ran off to the horizon, the grass more or less enclosed by a decomposing wire fence, buckling every few feet. Three bowed and broken wooden steps attached to the barn led up to a dusty, hay-strewn platform from which the barn doors hung open, sagging on their hinges.

Not a model agricultural unit. And not a living creature in sight.

I got out of the car and started for the steps. From out of nowhere a dog came bounding around the far corner of the barn, barking in a demented frenzy. A scruffy, mangy, muddy, wet mongrel. He stopped a few feet away, shook himself violently, spattering mud in all directions, rending the air with his barking.

A dog? Did that mean the place was inhabited? Or had he taken a little cross-country run from some neighboring house? In any case, how did he get so wet? It hadn't rained for days.

I watched him running in a small circle, wild with lunatic excitement, directly between me and the steps I wanted to climb. Who knew what he would take it into his head to do if I persisted? I had to get him out of the way. I bent down, picked up a pebble, and hoped it would work: it always did with George.

"Here!" I called, "fetch it!" and threw the pebble as far as I could.

Instantly, he sat down and shut up. Not what I had in mind, but if he stayed put, it would do. I took a step.

And a dozen filthy chickens appeared from somewhere, scrabbling across the dry dirt.

And human footsteps came shuffling up behind me.

I whirled around. A large, heavy, shapeless figure approached. It wore dirt-caked boots, coarse baggy pants stiff with grime, and a mildewed, mud-colored shirt that looked as though it had been chewed by rats. Above this a face of putty-colored skin was surrounded by a string mop of greasy gray hair. Anatomy proclaimed it female. It gave me a gap-toothed smile. I exerted heroic self-control and repressed a shudder.

"Did ya want somethin'?"

"I . . . was . . . driving by and saw the barn . . . I thought maybe it was for sale. I know someone who . . . wants to buy a barn."

"Ah-ha." She darted a sly glance at the barn and chuckled wheezily. "We don't look so good today. I got to clean up, but I been busy. I'm all alone, see. When the uncle was around it was different, but I'm all alone now. He died. And the old lady just sits in a chair, she don't move. I'm the only one. So . . . but it's a good little farm. Marie, she took off and got married somewheres. And Kevin . . . he's . . . I don't know *where* Kevin is. But I said, no, I'll stay with the uncle, I'll stay here and help out. So I been livin' here since I was little. But I got to clean up soon."

I edged toward the car. "Well, I'm sorry to have bothered you."

"You come back sometime after I clean up. We'll look a lot better. At least"—she pointed a thick, grubby finger at me—"at least we didn't give up. We stuck it out." She nodded, pleased with the way things had turned out. "We'll be all right."

I forced a smile. "Good-bye for now." I got into the car while she stood there with her caked lips parted over the black gaps between her grayish teeth, and made it back to the road in a little over a second.

If Dakin was concealed there, I thought, she'd be dead by now, from a dozen different diseases.

My small spurt of hope blighted, I drove on, my eyes raking the countryside for another likely cache between there and the camp, but the next few miles presented nothing of possible interest, no house, barn, shack, outhouse, rain barrel, cave, copse or hollow that could conceivably hide a small, state-of-the-art demagogue. And then I was at the camp.

It was busy. Clearly the weekend influx was under way; strange cars and vans standing amid the stubble, strange women wandering around the grounds and milling about the information booth, finding out that camping sites in the back meadow were limited by the camp's permit, gathering information about nearby campgrounds or trailer parks or lodgings. (There must be a state park somewhere, I thought vaguely.) The new people all looked eager, excited, restless. But the groups of regular campers, huddling together here and there in subdued conversation, looked as though they were holding a wake. The news had obviously spread: *The cops were here, they think we had something to do with it.*

It.

I drove up to the parking area, so programmed now to scan the horizon for a hiding place that I focused automatically on the burned-out farmhouse beyond the barn. It stood there, blind and apparently empty. Available, and exceedingly handy . . .

Well, well, well. The bluebird of happiness?

No, I told myself. No, it would be an inconceivable risk.

First of all, it was too accessible: while the back door was nailed shut, the front door was unlocked, campers could go in and out at will. Secondly, even if *they* had somehow locked the front door, half the ground-floor windows had no panes in them, and all it needed to break through the plasterboard that kept out the rain was a good hard poke with one of the garden implements. Tempting, too, on a rainy night.

On the other hand, a two-story house would have rooms upstairs, and those rooms would certainly have doors, and *those* doors could be locked. . . .

But sound carried across the campgrounds at night as though this were a Swiss mountain valley, and a prisoner would certainly be heard shouting. Even if they had her gagged, there would have to be times, when she ate or drank, that she could utter one strangled cry before they clapped a hand over her mouth.

119

Unless, of course, they kept her sedated. . . .

Sedated, since Tuesday night? Wouldn't that be dangerous? Maybe not. A very low dose, just enough to keep her groggy . . .

But no. No, not even *they* would have the nerve to keep her in the farmhouse, right here, on their own campgrounds!

Still . . . among the facts of life one stored away as a child was the discovery that the best place to hide something was right out in the open.

It wouldn't hurt to check it out. I had the eight-to-twelve shift tonight. I would just patrol myself over there.

I locked the car and went, warily, toward the barn. What was going on in there? None of the Unholy Five, I'd noticed, had been among the crowd at the gate: H-M's flame of hair most conspicuously absent. Were they all closeted in the main office, planning their defense? Doris in charge, armed with her legalities? Lotte sitting on the floor doing her calisthenics, getting ready to fight if they came for her? JoAnne looking frank and ingenuous, her mind teeming with subtle stratagems? Heath-Morecomb pacing back and forth, giving vent to histrionic bursts of invective? Harriet consulting her watch to see if it was time to look in on the captive?

I went in. Doris, at any rate, was not closeted. She was in the front office, speaking into the phone. She looked tense, but then I'd never seen Doris when she didn't look tense. Lightheartedness was not her strong suit. There were two new arrivals fidgeting around, waiting to ask questions, and Cynthia, the Ph.D. from Harvard, stood with her palms planted on the desk, listening to Doris's end of the conversation, her brow, normally as smooth as brown velvet, furrowed in thought.

"Look, we're busy here," Doris said into the phone, "we can't keep making comments all day long. We have nothing to say, it's none of our business."

I went through to the main barn area. Three of the regular campers were muttering unhappily in one of the

120

cubicles; a fourth wandered disconsolately toward the back of the barn. Dakin was causing more gloom by her absence than she ever had by arriving in the first place.

In the central office Harriet was at the desk, sorting anxiously through a stack of papers. As I walked in she whipped something off the desk into an open drawer, shut the drawer and looked up. The customary small, secret smile, I noticed, was not in evidence. She waited for me to speak.

"Trouble," I said, trying to suggest empathy.

"Nothing we can't handle."

"Well, I know it's just harassment, but that can be demoralizing. Wouldn't it be a relief if she just turned up, somewhere."

There was a pause while Harriet frowned and looked down at the papers. "Perhaps not. It might make things even worse."

"How could it?"

"There's no anticipating crowd psychology, but as long as she's missing, there are enough possible reasons for it that the odds are against their making trouble, but if she reappeared now there would be too much drama, she'd become the magnet for all kinds of unfocused emotion. Anything could happen."

Baloney, Harriet, I thought, and said nothing.

"So much work," she said, fussing with the papers, "all these people showing up."

"Can I help?"

"Mm. Why don't you see—um—Lotte. Or Doris."

She wanted me out. I watched her divide the papers into separate stacks. "Harriet—everything connected with the protest is, on principle, nonviolent. Is that right?"

Her eyes flew up, startled. "Absolutely." She looked down at the desk, then up again. "You're not planning . . . ?"

I shook my head, went to the doorway, and turned back. "Is Heath-Morecomb around?"

It took a moment for her to answer. "I'm not sure."

"JoAnne?"

She checked her watch. "I don't think so. She had an errand to take care of."

An errand. At six in the evening. An errand scheduled to be taken care of at a specific time. I left the barn and headed for the back meadow, silently cursing. A few minutes earlier and I might have seen her leave, might have been able to follow her.

I crawled into the tent, deposited my parcel of clothes. When would I find time to wash them and hang them on that community clothesline past the vegetable plot, with its peculiar assortment of under and outer garments in sizes ranging from minuscule to amazonian? I stretched out on the sleeping mat.

I could have followed JoAnne. I could follow her next time. Or H.-M. Or Harriet. Any of them. Why hadn't I thought of that earlier? All I had to do, instead of driving crazily around the countryside looking for pestilential farms where I could contract hepatitis or chicken fever or whatnot, was to watch them and follow them when they left the camp. Simple. Except that there were five of them and one of me. Science had concluded it was not possible to be in more than one place at any given time, and on the evidence it was probably a sound conclusion. All right, then, I would follow the next one I caught venturing out. And then the next one after that. One at a time.

It should only take a month or two.

Perhaps I could co-opt Brenda. Assuming I could ever get her away from Michael What'shisname's camera.

Damn Greenfield, anyway. So blind! Stark, raving blind!

I dismissed him from my mind. I made plans. Tomorrow morning, early, I would start watching them. In the meantime I'd get something to eat somewhere, do my patrol, and sometime in the night get over to that burned-out house.

I stared up the few inches to the top of my wind sock.

122

What was it, I wondered, that Harriet had so hurriedly swept from the desk top into the open drawer?

A little before eight, I splashed my face with cold water at the sink in the washhouse and went on patrol. For an hour or so in the darkening dusk I made the usual rounds, noting the new tents pitched beyond the familiar ones, strolling along the wooded boundary and back, watching the pale stars appear in the sky. Someone was playing a guitar again: plaintive, plucked notes in the soft, warm night. Spring had somehow turned to summer. By nine o'clock the sky was a dark purple, scented with the sweet, humid fragrance of honeysuckle, and a heavy yellow moon hung just above the trees of the woods, behind a black laciness of leaves. A sensual night, a night for languor and seduction. A night that belonged to the past. To a young, dreaming Maggie, with young bare shoulders and young, extravagant yearnings. In a world with no need for antinuclear protests.

Without warning, tears sprang to my eyes. I blinked them away. The youth was gone, the shoulders were older, the world was what it was, and Elliot was barely talking to me.

But for a moment there I'd felt it all, the mystery and magic, the inexpressible intoxication, and I realized with a stab of envy that this could be what Greenfield had temporarily rediscovered. It was certainly what was making Brenda prance around. Unquestionably what had sent some camper to the curtained privacy of that willow tree by the stream. In spite of the missiles next door. Or maybe because of them.

With an effort, I turned my mind to the problem at hand, took my eyes from the moon, and focused again on the burned-out farmhouse. It stood beyond what Doris called the latrine, in the shadows cast by a couple of maples, a two-minute sprint from the tented meadow I was patrolling. Sprinting, however, attracted attention. As would strolling, if the stroll took me away from my designated patrol section and I ran across Doris.

123

I waited until almost eleven, and made my way down to where Mariko's flashlight was bobbing around.

"I'm going to the john, Mariko. The wash-house," I added, not knowing which appellation was familiar to her. "The latrine."

"Yes, okay. Is still people walking."

There were, unfortunately. A solitary woman, here and there, on her way to bed, a little activity to and fro between the meadow and the john. I'd considered putting off the exploration until my stint was over, but being on patrol was the only excuse I could think of in the event of my being caught at the farmhouse: "I saw a light flashing around the house and came over to check it out."

I spent a minute in the wash-house, waiting for a camper to leave, then made my way through as much shadow as I could find to the near side of the house, circled it, confirmed that the plasterboard was intact on all the ground-floor windows, stepped carefully onto the strip of porch that ran across the front of the house, eliciting a moan from a warped floorboard, put out a hand to try the door, and realized that it was slightly ajar. Might never close properly again, in fact, having suffered some irreparable damage to its alignment during the calamity that had befallen the place.

I eased it open a little more and sidled into a narrow front hall. Doorways on either side led to empty rooms long since stripped of their furniture: in one, a meager fireplace in a wall blackened by soot or smoke; in the other, wires dangling from a hole in the ceiling where a light fixture had hung, and a large light patch on one of the wallpapered walls where something framed had formerly covered the repeated design of swans on a lake. From this room a door opened into a kitchen at the back of the house, its walls charred and water-damaged, the linoleum on the floor buckled, the oven door hanging by one hinge.

The rooms were far from spacious, but not quite mean:

a modest little farmhouse, probably kept clean and tidy until disaster struck. Now it smelled of mildew, dust and damp. The acrid stench of smoke from the fire had apparently dissipated over time. I went carefully up the stairway, first clutching the wooden banister until I felt it wobble, then staying close to the wall. I found the first bedroom door wide open.

A cracked wall mirror stood in one corner against the wall, a lumpy, once-sodden pillow lay on the floor, otherwise the room was bare and empty. A bathroom was next, no one in the tub. Another bare bedroom, larger, had only a crumpled, singed rug on the floor. I was fairly certain now that Dakin was not in this house: it felt empty. But there was one room left, at the end of the hall, the door partially closed. I pushed it open with the toe of my sneaker, shined the muted light of my flash, covered by my spread fingers, around the space, and discovered the only piece of furniture in the house: a cot. A narrow cot on which a thin, uncovered mattress sagged sadly in the middle. And something on the floor under it. Something the size and shape of a deck of playing cards.

I crouched down, reached under the cot and brought it out. An audio cassette. I held it close to the flashlight and lifted a finger to let a beam hit the label. Printed by hand was one word: BIZET. Taped from a disc onto a blank cassette. There was no dust on the plastic case.

I looked around the room carefully, but if there were any other signs of recent occupation, the light was too dim to show them to me. The only other thing I detected was the odor of smoke. Not the smoke, though, of an *old* fire. I went as quickly as possible down the stairs, out of the house and across to the back meadow, the cassette in my pocket.

As I brooded through my last hour of security duty, there was little doubt in my mind as to the ownership of the Bizet tape. A review of the alternative possibilities virtually confirmed it. What it was doing there was another matter. Even if the cabal had hidden their captive there initially, as a quick and simple solution until they'd found something more secure, they would hardly furnish her with entertainment. Perhaps they'd had to stand guard, one at a time, and this was a way of passing the time. Or perhaps the other sleepers in the barn loft objected to the British fiddle player's habit of listening to music at 2:00 A.M. and this was her sanctum away from home. Heath-Morecomb's Hideaway.

How that woman did leave her things scattered about. As though I'd conjured her out of the night, she appeared.

It was close to midnight when I saw the dark shape moving along the edge of the meadow. This time there was no heart-stopping clutch of fear; her hair caught the moonlight between one patch of shadow and the next, and I knew who it was. I doused my light, surveillance be damned, and followed at what I judged a safe distance. She was carrying something at her side, something that looked like a shopping bag. Food, possibly. A thermos, for the captive. The overalls and stocking mask to put on before she went in to see the woman. Halfway up the meadow she turned and walked unhesitatingly into the woods, with the familiarity of someone repeating an oft-traveled route. The spot might have been an intersection, with the street name on a post.

In among the trees she flicked on a light, and I saw it glinting fitfully up ahead as she moved. Without a thought for the ten minutes left to the end of my patrol, I moved out of the meadow and into the woods after her.

And a piercing shriek from Mariko's whistle split the night.

I froze. Another blast on the whistle. God! Damn!

I ran back, across the meadow, dodging around tents, down toward where Mariko's flashlight was waving frantically in the dark. Not that I had the slightest idea what I would do if confronted by an interloper with a knife.

By the time I got there three other campers, awakened and disoriented, were stumbling out of a tent that seemed

126

to be on fire, and Mariko was hopping daintily back and forth calling, "Watah! Watah!"

I turned instantly and ran toward the barn, only to meet Lotte lurching toward me with a pail of water. "Take it!" she said, "I get more," and ran off in her Dr. Dentons or whatever it was she was wearing.

Smoke was still billowing out of the tent, whose flap faced the sparse woods on that side of the meadow, running between the camp and, according to Doris, "someone's property." While two of the luckless campers held the flap open and wailed about wet bedrolls, I sloshed the contents of the pail into the opening, and the smoke diminished somewhat. Lotte arrived with another pail, then two more campers lugging a washtub between them, and soon there was nothing coming from the tent but an odor. The source of it lay on the floor between the bedrolls, something that looked like a blackened white candle.

"A smoke bomb," someone said sepulchrally.

Half the camp had awakened by then and come to stand around, voicing anger, annoyance, apprehension, according to temperament. Doris, arms folded over a surprising baby-doll nightie, said it was clear the perpetrator had come through from the adjoining property and thrown it from the cover of the trees. Someone else was certain it was a Dakin supporter. A third voice was of the opinion that this was only the start of a siege. Some Pollyanna piped up that it could have been worse, there was no real harm done.

No harm, I thought, trudging off to my tent. A minor incident. A mere interruption. A brief intrusion that just happened to interfere with the possible discovery of Dakin's whereabouts.

I went to bed. And Heath-Morecomb went wherever she was going, unhindered.

CHAPTER ELEVEN

MY EYES OPENED AT FIRST LIGHT, AND passed along the news that day was beginning and it was time to move. Dew on the grass, a faint yellow streak at the horizon of a pearl-gray sky, a clean, green smell. Within a quarter of an hour I was entering the woods at the point where, as far as I could judge, Heath-Morecomb had entered it the night before. Give or take a few yards, it was about where I'd originally gone through them looking for the stream.

I found the stream again. Unless she'd waded across it in the dead of night—a course that would give even the archadventuress pause—she must have followed the bank either to the right or left. To the right it led toward Hunegger Mills and civilization, such as it was. To the left it wound beyond the huge overhanging willow to unexplored territory. I turned left, followed the bank to—and through—the curtain of willow wands, paused for a moment inside its encircling laciness to savor the lovely, secret, green cloister it formed, and continued on, uneventfully, for a half mile or so, until, on a distant rise of land, a vaguely familiar shape appeared. Another half mile, losing sight of it from time to time behind intervening trees and bushes, and then I could see it clearly.

It was a side view of the squalid barn where the muddy dog had barked and the dirty chickens had scratched and the large, grubby, gray creature had smiled at me.

The stream went by it. And that, of course, was how the dog got wet.

I stood in the tall, daisy-dotted grass, staring at it. A dilapidated barn, little more than a mile from the camp as the crow flies and the stream runs. No one around but a defective slattern with barely enough wit to raise a few scrawny chickens for food. Whose silence could probably be bought with an implied threat, or a promise, or some fantastic story.

Was that where Heath-Morecomb had gone at midnight with her shopping bag? If whoever-it-was hadn't thrown that smoke bomb, I wouldn't have to guess. I could, of course, follow the stream until I was close enough to the farm, cut across the field and try once more to get into the barn, but if the dog barked and the woman came out, and if her lopsided mind saw me as a threat, there was always a chance she could wield a mean pitchfork. On the whole it would be wiser to get confirmation before running the risk.

I made my way back to the camp and my tent. The sun was up.

Squatting on my mat in the tent opening, breathing in the early-morning smell of dew-drenched grass and earth, nibbling crackers and swallowing thin coffee from the thermos I'd filled at the kitchen shack the night before, I watched and waited, ready to follow the first one of the Five who set foot outside the campgrounds.

At six-thirty Big Sheila stumbled her sleepy way to the john and back. A little before seven a truck rumbled along the road. Some twenty minutes later the first general stirrings of the day began in and around the tents. By eight o'clock my unrestricted view of the grounds was being interrupted by all the comings and goings, and I got to my feet. By ten I began to quarter the area halfway between the front and back of the meadow, trying to keep an eye on all possible exits simultaneously, and hoping that Greenfield, somewhere on the Mass. turnpike by now, was having trouble with his carburetor or gaskets or whatever it was.

Crossing between two rows of tents, I encountered Brenda.

"Hey," she said, tugging at the waistband of her shorts, "where've you been? You missed World War Three."

"When was it?"

"Yesterday, at the truck gate. They were bringing in troops. Truckloads. A bunch of us linked arms and spread across the entrance to keep them out. The MPs came out of the base, with helmets and sticks, the whole shmeer, to scatter us. I scattered. Fifteen girls got carted away."

"I saw the trucks, when I passed by, earlier."

"And before that the cops were here."

"I know."

"About H-M's hat?"

I nodded, my eyes scanning the grounds.

"Jesus, what about that? What do you think?"

"This is a very public place to discuss it."

"It *is*?" She looked around, her mouth gaping a little. "I thought this was *our* turf."

"Listen, Brenda, I want to talk to you, but I may have to leave at any minute—"

She threw up her hands. "Leave. Between you and Michael my whole ego's going to be destroyed."

"Why," I asked, moving to one side for a view of the barn, "what did he do?"

"Nothing," she said. "Zero. Zilch. He takes pictures,

130

that's what he does. All day long he takes pictures, and then at night he goes on the base and takes more pictures. He's *married* to that camera. The *shoot.* It's the whole world. 'That was a good shoot.' 'We've got to map out tomorrow's *shoot.*' 'I want to take a look at yesterday's *shoot.*' It's not enough he's got that eyepiece stuck in his eye all the time, he has to run the whole tape over again to see what he already saw. I told you about lost causes? Meet number three hundred and seven."

At the front of the barn someone was moving toward the parking lot. I craned my neck to see.

JoAnne!

"I have to go, Brenda." I ran an obstacle course across the meadow, reached the parking area just as JoAnne's dusty Buick started for the road, unlocked the Honda, got behind the wheel, and heard someone calling my name. Lotte appeared in the rearview mirror. If I continued to back out, would she move? Not her. She was waving both hands to stop me, and shouting my name. Deliberate obstruction, no question. She was there to see to it that JoAnne got away without being followed. Standing there in the path of the car as though planted and growing roots. I rolled down the window and shouted *"What?"*

"Phone call! Important!"

I turned off the ignition and closed my eyes. Oh, this was no mere chance. This was engineered, somehow. Somehow someone had arranged for someone else to call me at this precise moment and say it was important.

I got out, slammed the Honda door and went to the barn, Lotte a few determined steps behind me. "Who is it?"

"Sounds to me like a man."

A man? Elliot? All the way from Tulsa?

"In the big office," she said, following to make sure I got there.

I picked up the phone. "Elliot?"

"No," said Greenfield's voice. "Are you busy?"

I breathed slowly in, and slowly out. "Where did you break down, Charlie?"

After a moment's silence he said, "As far as I can tell I am still whole, neither unnerved nor asthenic. There's no evidence of a breakdown."

"I mean the car."

"The car, when I left it in the hotel lot a few minutes ago, was fine. I'm using Julius's telephone. How soon can you get here?"

Only fear of being stopped for speeding on Padua's sedate streets kept me from doing more than a relatively innocent five miles over the limit.

So, he was still here. Or had he started out and come back? Was this a temporary postponement? A fundamental change of heart? I was so preoccupied with the possible implications of Greenfield's failure to be en route to Marlboro that JoAnne's Buick coming toward me on the avenue almost passed unnoticed.

I swung abruptly into the parking entrance of a lighting-fixture showroom, out again by the exit, and up the avenue instead of down, separated only by two sparkling clean cars from the Buick's smeary back end. JoAnne was keeping to the right, creeping along as though she were checking the storefront numbers for an address. Both sparkling cars eventually passed her. I kept my distance. At the second intersection she turned slowly into a residential street and stopped at the far end of the block. Dawdling along behind, I watched her leave the car and go up the walk to a Federal-style house, freshly painted pale blue with white trim and black shutters, neat lawn, clipped hedge, and a shiny brass plate on the wall next to the immaculately white front door. She pushed a bell, opened the door and walked in.

There was no telling, of course, how long she'd be in there, and I couldn't wait endlessly, not knowing what Greenfield was up to. On the other hand, JoAnne was suspect, and if she wasn't here on camp business, whatever she was doing could prove, at the very least, instructive.

I pulled in to the curb. Behind me, near the corner of the boulevard, a large, white, prosperous-looking church stood behind a wide, well-kept lawn, and on the lawn groups of women were standing around, chatting and smiling with ladylike gusto: some bazaar or charity affair going on inside, no doubt. I left the car, crossed the road and approached a group of four who were happily busy not listening to one another. One of them finally noticed me standing there and waited politely for me to state my business.

"Excuse me, I'm looking for a Webster Avenue. . . ."

At the sound of a foreign tongue the other three simultaneously ceased talking and turned their eyes on me.

"*Web*ster?"

"*Web*ster!"

"Never heard of it."

"There's a Washburn," one of them said, "but I've lived here all my life and there's never been a Webster."

She was the one I wanted.

"I was told Webster," I said to this one, "unless I heard wrong. I'll just have to make a call. Thank you." I smiled warmly. "This is a lovely neighborhood. Such pretty houses."

"If you want to see beautiful houses," said the woman who'd lived here all her life, "you want to take a look at Dunlop Road."

"If they're better than these, they must be magnificent. That pale blue one over there, for instance, with the black shutters—"

"Oh, that's Dr. and Mrs. Trachner's. He has his office there, too. Cardiology."

"Oh. Well, it's a charming house. Thanks very much. Sorry to bother you."

"You go see Dunlop Road," the lifelong native instructed me as I went off. "You'll really see something."

A doctor, I thought, back in the car, circling the block and heading back down the avenue. Pills. Drugs. Advice.

133

One of the campers? But hadn't the camp arranged for some doctor to be on call . . . ?

When I reached the Plaza I went into the bar. "He's upstairs," Julius told me. What, I wondered, was he *making* of all this? He still beamed whenever he saw me.

I put a dollar bill on the counter. "Julius, I can't keep using your phone without paying for it."

He grinned. "You'll never get rich that way," he said, and brought out the phone from under the counter. "Mr. Greenfield"—a shy, sideways glance—"says you work for him."

"It's true."

"Good." He chuckled and gave me the phone. "Then I've still got a chance."

Oh Lord. *Et tu, Julius.* I gave him an ambiguous smile, dialed the camp number and asked for Brenda.

"What's going on?" she asked when she came on the line. "The last person who ran out on me that fast was my landlord. I didn't ask *you* for heat."

"Brenda, does the camp have a doctor on call?"

"Are you *sick?*" Her voice, never exactly dulcet, made the phone vibrate.

"Keep it low, would you? No, I'm not sick. I just want to know his name."

"They've got it in the infirmary"—a hoarse croak was her effort at keeping it low—"you want me to check?"

"If you can do it without trumpets and cymbals."

Clattering and murmuring in the background while she was gone, and then she was back. "Norris," she confided in a stentorian whisper. I thanked her, promised details at a later date, hoped as I hung up that no one in the office had paid attention to the melodrama, and went upstairs to room number nine.

"Norris" was definitely not "Trachner."

CHAPTER TWELVE

GREENFIELD WAS STANDING AT THE FOOT OF the far bed looking down at a sea of paper that covered the entire bedspread. In the nineteen hours since I'd left him, his long face had somehow grown perceptibly longer, his gray hair grayer. The élan of the bon vivant had given way to the sobriety of the Supreme Court. Intoxication replaced by circumspection. He was even wearing a plain oatmeal-colored shirt.

Was it possible he'd been thinking it over and decided I was right? That was too much to hope for.

I said, carefully, "You look peaky. Why aren't you in Marlboro?"

He picked up one of the printed sheets covering the bed and studied it. "I think you could make an educated guess, if you tried."

I chanced it. "Well . . . I'd say you're in pain because you realize you're wrong about this mess."

He looked up, mildly astonished. "Wrong?" He looked back at the paper. "Being wrong is not the problem. The problem is that I have to spend too much valuable time proving I'm right."

I should have known.

"Why bother?" I waved aside the courtesy. "If you're right, I'll find out in due course. Don't waste valuable time proving it to me."

"It's not you I have to convince."

Not me? Himself? There was no one else around.

"You mean," I said, trying to nail it down, "you know you're right, but nevertheless the icy finger of doubt reached out in the night and touched you."

It was always when you most wanted a direct answer that Greenfield came up with a circumlocution. This one was a dilly.

"According to Cartesian philosophy," he said, "the only thing that's doubtless is doubt itself."

I waited, but apparently that was the whole reply.

"Does that mean," I asked, enunciating clearly, "you have doubts about Heath-Morecomb?"

"No. But I have doubts."

"About *what*?"

"I doubt the local authorities have ever read Descartes."

"Charlie, I don't know what you're saying."

"Descartes"—with conspicuous patience—"proposed the use of deduction and logic to counteract illusion."

"Ha! What do you think *I've* been proposing?"

His look made it clear that Descartes and I in no way inhabited the same world. "The proposition is only valid," he said, "when you know which illusion you're fighting. I don't trust the authorities to pinpoint the real illusion. *You* haven't." He gestured to the bed. "I've been to the *Ledger* offices. They ran off some copies for me. Your protest apparently rates daily coverage."

I looked down at the bed. Print and pictures in all directions. There were dates for virtually every day in the past three months: WOMEN'S ENCAMPMENT PLANNED ON SITE OF FORMER KEANS FARM, PROTESTERS SEEK HARMONY WITH COMMUNITY, OFFICIALS MEET TO DISCUSS WOMEN'S CAMP, INCIDENT AT HUNEGGER BASE. Pictures of the campgrounds, of women in front of the main gate, chanting, of banners with slogans, of guards in uniforms.

I dismissed it all. "You've gone to a lot of trouble for nothing, Charlie. I think I know where Dakin is."

He looked at me from under the bristling eyebrows: a devout nonbeliever. I told him about the farm with the dog, the chickens and the Creature. I described Heath-Morecomb's midnight skulking through the woods and my exploratory morning check of the route she'd obviously taken. I explained my reasoning. I waited for acknowledgments that I might have a point.

He picked up one of the *Ledger* copies and handed it to me. It was a shot of local citizens watching a group of women sitting on the ground in front of the main entrance to the base, giving voice. Guards behind the fence, also watching. A profile view of a female figure, standing, playing a violin. On the ground at her feet a straw boater with a lettered band around the crown.

"Not a flattering picture," I said.

"Examine it."

"I don't have to. It's almost a replica of what I saw at the gate the night I got here. Except that it's dated the Friday before that. Is it supposed to be significant?"

"The hat is on the ground."

I agreed. "The hat is on the ground. The hat was also on the ground when I saw her the following Monday night. She seems to be in the habit of dropping it on the ground and then picking it up and putting it on. But then, she's an artist: they're not required to be fastidious."

He ignored that. "And there are a number of people in that picture within reach of that hat."

I shook the picture impatiently. "This was Friday night,

137

Charlie. The following Monday night the band was still on the hat."

"You're missing my point, *and* your own: she was in the habit of dropping the hat on the ground. Therefore she made it accessible to anyone standing around, at *any* time."

"Anytime doesn't count. Tuesday night is what counts, and she not only had it Monday night but I saw her wearing it Tuesday afternoo . . ."

"Do you have a toothache, or are you going to be sick?"

I took my hand from my lips. The involuntary gesture had been a response to something I'd remembered. Something I'd forgotten until now. (Or chosen to forget? I preferred not to believe that.) Now the image of Heath-Morecomb in the barn on Tuesday, kneeling on the canvas, wearing the hat, flashed across my inner eye.

"She was wearing the hat," I murmured, "on Tuesday. But now that I think about it . . ."

He watched me struggle for a while before he supplied the unspoken words. "The band was missing."

I nodded.

"On Tuesday afternoon," he added.

"That doesn't necessarily mean it was lost! Or that anyone took it!"

"It was gone, Maggie. You've chosen your hypothesis, I'll choose mine. Give that Friday night picture a second scrutiny. If some of those townspeople were there again on Monday night, it's possible you'll remember seeing them."

"Possible," I said dryly, "but not likely." Monday night at the gate I'd been in shock, I'd traveled a long route to get away from the consequences of Heath-Morecomb's visit, only to find her finally ensconced in the place to which I'd fled. I hadn't been in any condition to take note of onlookers.

However, I stared dutifully at the picture in my hand. The only thing I noticed in that "second scrutiny" was that among the faces of the local citizens standing on the sidelines there was a familiar one. Two, in fact.

"I see a couple of familiar faces, but not because I saw them at the gate." I pointed them out. "That's the woman I told you about, who thinks we're all terrorists, the one who was at the Dakin press thing, the one who held up the line at the gas station. The woman next to her is her friend, the one she told about the extra troops being brought in."

He took the picture from me and studied it. "Do you know anything about this woman? The one who knew about the troops?"

"How should I? She's a resident of Padua. Class of '54. Ethel something. What's the difference?"

"What does she have to do with Dakin's outfit?"

"Just a disciple, as far as I know. She could have been on the local coordinating committee." It seemed to me there'd been a name like *Ethel* on the list I'd made for the Brain Trust.

"See what you can find out about her."

"About *her?*" Why?"

He placed the newspaper cut carefully on the bed. "Because," he said quietly, "she's angry, and she's connected, if peripherally. The consequences of a crime reverberate in the lives of those it affects. Those people keep moving, and their movements can be revealing. The only hope we have of discovering anything significant—and that hope is so slender it's virtually invisible—is to probe, watch, and listen. And we have to start somewhere."

"Charlie, for God's sake, why should this woman Ethel be connected with Dakin's disappearance? She's on *Dakin's* side. She was *delighted* to have her come here from Dubuque or wherever. She *wants* her to fight the camp. Dakin is Ethel's spokeswoman. Possibly her patron saint. I wouldn't be surprised if Ethel faces the Midwest when she prays."

"Precisely."

Precisely!

I marched to the door. "I don't have time for the Descartes method, Charlie. The barn with the dog and the chickens may be the wrong illusion, but our British friend was going *somewhere* last night and the banks of that stream are not littered with convenient hiding places. And it was no illusion that JoAnne, who is perfectly healthy, ran off to consult a doctor who is *not* the camp doctor, which to me means that JoAnne is worried about someone outside the camp who is not too well, and that worries me because if Dakin expires this is going to get *very* serious, so—"

"When did that happen?"

"About an hour ago. So if you really want to get to the bottom of this, you can come with me to check out that barn. If not, then *you* find out about Ethel, because what I have to do is urgent."

He looked at his watch, ran his hand over his face. "I'll make allowance for the fact that your thinking is skewed by a prejudice."

My thinking!

"How far is this barn?"

"Not far." I hadn't really expected him to come. "About a mile from the camp, on a road that goes by the base."

He shuffled the *Ledger* copies on the bed into a pile. "There's no point in taking two cars. When we get this out of the way, you can drop me and get to work."

When you're winning, you don't pick an argument, and I was fairly certain there would be no need for further investigation after the barn, but I couldn't resist.

"And after we get the barn *out of the way*," I said, "what are *you* going to be doing?"

He ran a hand over his face. "Maggie. A woman I've never met disappeared from the grounds of a base I've never seen, while presumably on her way back to an inn with which I'm not acquainted, having been abducted, you say, by members of a camp of which I'm virtually ignorant, in a town with which I'm almost totally unfamiliar. The choices are infinite."

A direct answer? Maybe in the next life.

We went out of the room, down the stairs, out to the street and around the side of the hotel to where the Honda was parked. Greenfield, flagrantly patient, inserted himself in the passenger seat as I got behind the wheel.

I took a shortcut.

If a flyspeck of a village the size of Hunegger Mills can be said to have outskirts, I drove through them to reach the road to the dilapidated farmyard I'd visited the day before.

"Dakin's car," I told Greenfield, "was found somewhere around here. I don't know exactly where. On a back road near the village was all I was told."

"Mm," he said. "Perhaps, with the application of thumbscrews, you might find out *which* back road. When it comes to information, we're hardly laboring under an embarrassment of riches."

"I don't think you're allowed to use thumbscrews on the police. Besides, I thought, it won't be necessary."

I trundled over the little iron bridge and glanced for brief respite at the daylilies on the bank of the stream. Greenfield glanced at his watch. Again.

"Are you timing something?"

"I have an appointment in forty minutes."

An appointment. To tell her Marlboro was off.

"With someone on the base," he added.

"*On* the *base!*"

"I arranged it this morning, by phone. Maggie, this is a field full of weeds. The road is to your left."

I was *barely* off the road. "But how—who— You can't just *call* an Air Force base! What do you say to them? 'You don't know me but I want to come in and look at your missiles'?"

"I'm not entirely unknown in military circles."

It should not have been a surprise. Greenfield had an unparochial acquaintanceship that ranged from Soviet emigré musicians and mandarin columnists for the *Manchester Guardian* to a fish farmer in Idaho and a dissolute

141

expatriate barfly in the Yucatán. Why not a wing commander? Still—

"You know someone at the base and you didn't tell me?"

He shifted in the seat, trying to find some rapport between his long legs and the short space. "It's a recent acquisition, roughly two hours old. The source goes back forty years."

He stared out at the fields, seeing something else.

"What source?"

"The last world disaster." He was long-winded only when you didn't want him to be.

"And? What happened that led to this?"

He looked at me. "Are you making conversation?"

"I like to learn things. Also, I'm nervous."

He sighed. "I was sent, on behalf of the *Stars and Stripes,* to interview a fighter pilot. His plane had been crippled by enemy fire over Normandy, came down near Rennes where the Germans were already thin on the ground, most of them having left to protect their flank farther east. The pilot managed to escape and crawled into the back of a bakery van that somehow ended up in Bordeaux. He'd been listed as missing in action, but eventually he turned up in Paris with twelve double magnums of Lafite Rothschild, given to him, he said, by the vintner himself. It was one of those episodes beloved of men who like to think of war as a series of men's club stories. It did not appeal to me. The first thing the pilot said to me was, 'Are you going to write one of those *cute* things?' I realized he was a thinking human being and we became friendly. He became a colonel. I tracked him down and asked him if he knew anyone at Hunegger. He has, it turned out, a nephew who is chief of public affairs at the base. Is that enough?"

I shook my head in wonderment. "Wasn't it you who said military intelligence is a meaningless phrase because the two words are mutually exclusive?"

"Only a fool chooses his acquaintances on the basis of categories rather than individual character."

Really. And how did you come to mess up on the British acquaintance?

I didn't say it, of course. For one thing, the barn had come into view.

"Is that it?" he asked, with as much curiosity as if he were sighting another Travel Lodge.

"That's it." From this angle the ramshackle gray barn listed slightly to one side on its rise of land. I felt my stomach knot with apprehension. All very well to suspect, explore, deduce, and go haring off to the rescue, but there would be obstacles, there would be complications. . . . Greenfield, as he often did, read my mind.

"What will we do about the dim-witted female?" he asked. "Confuse her with fast talk?"

"And grab the pitchfork fast."

"What about muzzling the dog? Or do we shoot him?"

"I know how to handle him." Well, sort of.

I turned cautiously into the track, up the rise and around to the back of the barn. Neither dog nor chickens were in evidence, and the Creature was nowhere on the horizon. We left the car, walked across the pebbled dirt, climbed the spavined wooden stairs to the platform and looked around.

In a shadowy corner formed by a moldering wall and one of the dangling barn doors lay a pile of dirty sacking. A hoe with crumbs of dried earth adhering to it had been left lying on the floorboards amid nameless droppings. A rusting pail hung on some inner wall beyond a door-size opening at the far end of the platform. Greenfield looked with profound distaste at the hoe, reluctantly took a handkerchief from his pocket, picked up the tip of the handle and poked at the sacking. There was nothing under it but the dusty floorboards strewn with shreds of hay.

The opening at the other end of the platform led to three wooden stairs that descended to a short corridor in which a closed door in the outer wall beckoned, grimly. Remembering the exterior arrangements, I thought I knew what stood behind it. Greenfield, ahead of me, had stopped to consider a padlock hanging unfastened from its hasp. A padlock on a silo? There had to be a strange reason for that. A prisoner, for instance. The door could be opened for air when all was quiet, locked if there were prying eyes around. Why it was both closed and unlocked I didn't bother to speculate, because Greenfield was opening the door.

A musty cylinder smelling of decaying vegetable matter rose to a height of twenty feet or so, a rung ladder climbing the concave wall to the top like someone desperate to escape. The top of the silo, though, was lost in shadow, the lid was on, and only the oblique light inside the barn showed us the three-foot-high stack of corn ears growing brown at the bottom of it. Greenfield was about to shut the door again, but I held it open, stubbornly staring at the pile of corn.

"The hoe," I mouthed, inclining my head toward the platform.

He turned away: clearly the suggestion was too macabre to be taken seriously. I took the handkerchief from his hand, went back for the hoe, and moved the corn back and forth to no avail. I upended the hoe and poked the handle through the cobs in a dozen different places, detecting nothing in the process but more cobs, while Greenfield stood by looking like a geophysicist watching a high school science class.

We moved on, and into a small room with rough plaster walls, in which an enormous white porcelain vat, astoundingly clean, occupied nine-tenths of the space: a mammoth, windowless, doorless washing machine. I looked at it and then at Greenfield, brazening it out. With a glance of unmistakable despair for my lurid imagination, he examined the machine, worked a lever that lifted the lid, looked in, lowered the lid, and said quietly and with unconcealed satisfaction, "Milk."

Milk?

There were two dingy doors leading out of the room. One, which I opened with the hand that still held Greenfield's handkerchief, showed me the dirt track. Greenfield opened the other and closed it again, looking repelled.

"*What?*" I whispered.

"You don't want to go in there."

"*Why?*"

"*I* don't want to go in there."

"Charlie—" I tried to squeeze past him. He stopped me with a hand, opened the door wide.

As far as the eye could see—cows. Large, smelly, filthy, dun-colored, slack-jawed, glassy-eyed, catatonic bovine animals, herded together, flank to flank, with scarcely enough room between them for the flies and ticks and God-knows-what that crawled about. I shuddered.

MILK IS GOOD FOR YOU.

What were they doing indoors? Why weren't they out in some green pasture looking serene and pastoral from a distance?

Well, they weren't. They were here, and we were going to have to go through them, or around them. Massed together for some reason in two-thirds of the available space, they left a margin some three feet wide between their brown flanks and three of the walls. Ample space to hide a woman. It was too late, of course: if Dakin was in there she had already died of the stench. Nevertheless I poked at Greenfield, urging him on. He looked at the cows rumbling and lowing and shuffling and swishing tails and dribbling. Through the murmurous miasma, he said, "This is an exercise in empty masochism. There is no abductor on earth inhumane enough to hide his victim in this place." But he went, and I followed, holding my breath.

Treading on undefinable grit and an occasional masticated corncob, we proceeded clockwise around the fetid area, until, just ahead of Greenfield, between two waist-high partitions, I caught sight of what looked like a shopping bag.

Heath-Morecomb, at midnight, heading for the woods with a shopping bag.

I nudged him, and pointed, and at that moment the doorway through which we'd come was suddenly and massively filled by a ponderous, dreary apparition that was only too familiar. She spotted us immediately—not so bloody slow, the Creature—but decided to talk to the cows first.

"You didn't do so good today," she told them in her uninflected, disconnected way. "You got to do better, hear me? The old lady's talking crazy again, I got other things to do. Get those flies off. Hear me? Clean yourself up. We got to get this place tidy."

Greenfield, after his initial moment of incredulity, started back in her direction, but whatever plan he had in mind was forestalled by her next words, addressed directly to him. "You one of them? The old lady don't like them, and she's talking crazy again. Tell them to go away, she says, I don't like policemen. What did you come in here for?"

At his most falsely benign, Greenfield said, "Could you tell me where the police are now?"

She looked at him suspiciously, then suddenly gave him the full force of her gap-toothed smile. Stoic that he was, his gaze never wavered.

"Down by the stream," she said, "down past the cornfield. Whole bunch of them. I had to call them, 'cause she wouldn't move. I told her she couldn't sleep there, but she wouldn't move. That's Jubiler property, belongs to my uncle. He's dead now, there's only me. And the old lady, but she—"

"The old lady wouldn't move?"

"No, the old lady's in the *house*. There was somebody down by the stream. Sleeping there. I told her—"

"Which way is the cornfield?"

She pointed toward Hunegger Mills. "Starts near the road and goes to the stream. It's all flat there, for growing things. You can see it all from the house. That's why—"

146

But by then we were past her, through the doorway, through the room with the vat, and Greenfield was opening the door onto the dirt track.

I drove toward Hunegger while Greenfield looked for corn stalks and police cars, neither of which were apparent from the road. We were nearing the iron bridge and I'd decided we'd missed the place, when I saw the two cars from the sheriff's department parked on the bank where I'd stopped to look at the daylilies. A deputy leaned against the side of the first vehicle, talking into the mike of his three-way radio. On the opposite bank, on the far side of the bridge, two old men, one barrel-shaped woman and an adolescent boy with a nose peeling from sunburn stood watching him.

I drove across the bridge, stopped on the verge just past the group of villagers, and we walked over to where they stood.

"I've been telling them for years this place wasn't safe," one of the old men was saying.

"Nobody could fall in that stream accidentally," the boy said, "in the *daytime*. Unless they were *blind*."

"Has there been an accident?" Greenfield asked, idly curious.

"Found a woman downstream," the other old man said, unperturbed. "Full of water as a potato."

The barrel-shaped woman, arms crossed over her shelf of flowered polyester, said importantly, "That woman who was missing, on the radio. They've been saying on the radio she was missing. You'd think they'd have found her before this."

"Drowned?" I managed to ask.

The first old man gave me an answer of sorts. "Well, she's dead, anyhow."

CHAPTER THIRTEEN

REENFIELD SAT IN THE HONDA STARING AT the village street ahead that wound past the laundromat and the Mills Café and the hardware store with its rakes and bags of fertilizer and stiff American flag in the window. I sat beside him, my mind numb. Dakin was dead. The nightmare had materialized. I could think of no reasonable response to it.

"She died in the barn," I said dully, "and they dumped her in the stream."

"The only bodies," he said, "that travel from downstream to upstream are those belonging to salmon, and they're unique—and alive. I grant you, that cow shack is scabrous and mephitic enough to wipe out an entire nation in a week, all they'd have to do is bottle it. But the woman pointed upstream to indicate where she found Dakin. This

148

—is upstream. If the water carried the body down, then *this* is where the body entered it."

I struggled with that. Could Heath-Morecomb, last night, have taken the path in the opposite direction, toward some other hiding place, here in Hunegger?

Greenfield consulted his watch. "I have an appointment in five minutes. There's no time to go back for my car. You'll have to drop me at the entrance to the base. I'll get myself back to the hotel when I'm finished there."

I stared at him. "Charlie—"

He indicated the key in my hand, and then the ignition, and while I drove, he slumped in the seat, his chin pushing up into his lower lip—a realignment of his features with which he customarily greeted serious trouble. "The sooner you begin collecting information—*any* information— about anything in connection with anyone hostile to the camp—"

"You mean two-thirds of the local population?"

"Start with the obvious ones."

"My God! Apart from the numbers, where's the Cartesian logic? Would the Yankees kill their star pitcher?"

"We don't know she was murdered."

"True. She could have been out picking blueberries and slipped. She could have put her own head in the water because she'd had a message from her own personal God that Gabriel was retiring and the position was open. She—"

"There are less whimsical possibilities."

"Yes indeed. One in particular."

He sat up, a gesture of terminal exasperation. "Someone planted that hatband in Dakin's car to implicate someone from the camp. Does that suggest anything to you?"

It did. Oh, it did. It strongly suggested that I was once again talking to the wind. It was H.-M.'s hatband. H.-M. had been at the base when Dakin disappeared. H.-M. had stolen through the woods at midnight to the stream where Dakin was subsequently found. But Greenfield was not a man to be daunted by the force of evidence. He was not going to abandon a diagnosis of fractured tibia simply because blood was pouring from a severed hand.

I pulled up at the main gate to the base. There was the usual activity, the usual civilian contingent watching it. Greenfield took a slip of paper from his pocket, pushed up his sunglasses with a thumb, and squinted at it. "I have to ask the guard to call Lieutenant Colonel Harwood." He dropped the glasses, pocketed the slip. "He will collect me, show me around, and see to it that I don't sneak off to pilfer any top-secret blueprints. In the meantime, of course, the vetted and vouched-for man in the research lab is on the Libyan payroll." He looked at my face, which evidently expressed something far from hilarity.

"Transcending depression," he said, "is your *other* assignment." He gestured to the clutch of men and women with their eyes riveted on the protesters at the gate. "Start digging."

"With what?"

The eyebrows rose, two grizzled birds taking off in opposite directions. "With the only available tool. A divining rod." He went off to the guard shack, spoke with the unsmiling young guard in the beret, who went back into his cubicle, reappeared, said something, and stood waiting beside Greenfield. I also waited, partly to put off my impossible task, partly to be certain Greenfield did actually get past the gate.

A dark blue compact drove up to the shack from the base grounds and a tall, rangy officer got out, flashed a smile, shook Greenfield's hand and held the door for him to get into the car.

Typical, I thought. When I went on the base, I got a major with a head cold. Greenfield got a lieutenant colonel with so much charm you could feel it from the curb.

I started the car.

Where was I going?

I sat there for a while, forcing myself to believe there was good reason to start ferreting among the antagonists. *If,* I told myself, *if* there's a chance the hatband was planted, then this Ethel person is as good a candidate as any. She had the opportunity. She certainly had the motive. She'd behaved peculiarly, with the charge card at the gas station. There was also the suggestion she'd taken a trip she denied having taken, to Schenectady. Her personality was by no means at odds with the idea of a scheming woman. I could easily imagine her being insidious and persuasive: a female Iago, with a blackjack as backup. She could have wriggled close to Dakin, enlisted her cooperation in a coup that went wrong. But wrong how? And why?

It was too murky, too mobile. It wouldn't stand still. Details were easier. Ethel who? Ethel what?

If she *had* been on the coordinating committee, her name would be on the list I'd made at the press briefing, but the list was somewhere in the camp office and if I asked for it, someone would want to know why. I still hadn't been cleared for *absolute trust*.

I drove into Padua to one of the few places I knew. Gas stations have telephones, therefore directories. My gum-chewer was not there. I went into the office and in answer to my request received a soiled, dog-eared book from a black-browed man who looked as though he were giving the world ten seconds to shape up. I looked up the *Padua Ledger* and asked the man humbly for directions.

The *Ledger* offices occupied a storefront building in the central shopping mall, the quarters so featureless I'd neglected to notice them on Tuesday, when I'd bought my notebook and take-away salad in the nearby supermarket. Behind an uncompromising counter that acted as a barrier between visitor and personnel, assorted news slaves sat at cluttered desks bearing not only typewriters and telephones, but a real word processor or two. At the *Reporter* in Sloan's Ford, the four of us were still struggling with eyeshades and quill pens. A hollow-cheeked young man in a limp shirt looked up at me as though I were the last straw on his beleaguered back, and came reluctantly to the counter.

"I'd like to buy a back copy of the *Ledger,* dated last Tuesday."

He sighed. I'd asked for the moon. "I'll see if we have any," he moaned, and disappeared, to return almost immediately with the paper. It had been an arduous task. I took the paper out to the Honda and went through it, checking the items page by page. On page seven I found a picture: six middle-aged people aiming their fixed smiles at the camera on a lawn outside the Sycamore Inn. CLASS REUNION CELEBRATED AT SYCAMORE.

Sprague, it said below. Ethel Sprague, between two hearty-looking men. The other classmates apparently camera-shy or otherwise engaged. Including Ethel's friend in the knit suit and imitation pearls, who'd probably been busy ransacking her bag for lipstick or pillbox. I folded the paper, went into the supermarket and over to the checkout counter, where a pale plump girl with smudged blue eyeliner directed me to the public phone. Another directory in hand, I found a D. Sprague on Linden, and an R. Sprague on Westover.

I remembered the real estate office opposite the gas station, drove back to the boulevard, and after parrying the unstoppable sales pitch of an avid young agent resolved to sell me an entire city block of Padua, emerged with an appointment for the following Monday to view a property in the north end of town that had been put on the market by one Roy Sprague. I'd also managed to snare a street map.

The house, first.

I studied the map, and drove north on the boulevard, then west, wondering if my mother down in her island paradise would be amused or annoyed that I'd given the agent her name as my own for an appointment I would never keep.

On Westover, a street of Puritan rectitude so unassailable you had the feeling that terrible things must go on behind those starched lawns and corseted bricks, I found the Sprague house, a tightfisted vertical shoe box, with the slatted blinds closed against the sun and a token azalea in a terra-cotta pot on the front porch. I rang the bell and waited, without much hope: there was no white Chevy in the driveway, no other car behind the small glass window of the garage door. Three rings, three waits, and I left, and drove back to the boulevard.

The north end of it was clearly not Padua's best real estate buy—older, narrower, without either the sterile gleam to the south or the antique appeal of Julius's neighborhood. The Sprague property, Pens 'n' Papers, was a stationery-and-greeting-card store, a little the worse for twenty years or so of declining business. Happy Birthday, Mom, Dad, Great-Uncle, Brother-in-Law. Primary-color cartoons of gray-haired ladies in bikinis: You're Only as Old as Your Bathing Suit. There were newspapers and magazines on a rack, cigars, cigarettes, flashlight batteries, even a desperate Lottery window. An old woman like a rheumatoid sandpiper was picking through the choice of gift wrappings, and a stout, gloomy man with a pendulous lower lip was rearranging the stacks of manila envelopes as though they were his life's accumulated mistakes.

I interrupted him. "Mr. Sprague?"

He turned his heavy face in my direction, the eyes dead, incurious, and inclined his head a quarter of an inch.

"I'm looking for Mrs. Sprague."

"She's not here."

"Do you know where I might find her?"

He shrugged. "She's probably not home. She goes out in the afternoon. What's it about?"

"I wanted to interview her as a possible subject for a book I'm writing."

The drooping eyelids lifted lethargically, to denote astonishment.

"It's a sort of social history, called 'Twenty Years Later.' The idea is to take four diverse sections of the country and record the changes that have occurred in the lives of a half-dozen representative people of a given area over a span of twenty years. In this case we've decided to choose the subjects from among the Community College class of '54."

"Are you going to pay her?"

I cleared my throat. The real wonder of the human body is that with all its miraculous propensities, the most sensitive aperture is still the pocket it wears on the outside. I said, "Well, naturally. If we decide on her as a subject."

"She's usually home around six," he said hopefully.

I frowned, trying to look important and busy in my rumpled, cow-smelling jeans. "My time here is limited. You have no idea where she might have gone?"

"Well." He breathed once, like a damaged bellows. "You know. She goes shopping. I guess."

The old woman approached the cash register on legs burdened by age and gentility, holding a long roll of wrapping paper, pink and blue nosegays on an eggshell background. Mr. Sprague was torn between a windfall of financially interesting potential and a definite sale of two dollars and thirty-five cents. I put an end to his anguish.

"I'll call her at six," I said, and left the store.

Of course there was no such leeway in my schedule. By six the whole town would know about Dakin, and it would take an injection of truth serum to get even superficial information from anyone. I sat in the car, pondering. Mr. Sprague apparently knew little about his wife's social habits, but there was someone who might know more. The trouble was she hadn't been photographed by the *Ledger* and therefore her name didn't appear there. "Connie" I'd dredged up from memory, but people were not listed that way in the directories. And I'd burned that bridge as far as Mr. Sprague was concerned. If this social historian I was supposed to be, so pressed for time, were to ask for a list of Ethel's friends, with the implication of hours to be spent tracking her down, there would be no credibility left worth mentioning.

There was just one slim chance.

I went back into Pens 'n' Papers and once again asked for a telephone book. Three bridal shops were listed in the yellow pages, one per thousand of population. Weddings were a major activity in Padua. I copied down all three addresses, consulted the map. I found Bea's Bridal Salon (*Gowns, Formal Wear, Invitations,* and—either hope or cynicism—*Second Marriages*) at the south end of the boulevard, next to a liquor store.

A confection of white rattan furniture and gilt-framed photographs of puppetized brides, against a background of salmon-pink walls. A well-upholstered matron in aqua satin regarding herself dubiously in a long mirror, and a thin woman with pursed mouth tugging gently at a recalcitrant sleeve.

"It looked better at the last fitting," said aqua satin woefully.

"It looks fine. It really looks perfect. I wouldn't touch it."

"It pulls. Across here."

Pursed-mouth drew her nonexistent eyebrows together. "Well, I can *try* moving that seam a quarter of an inch. I can't promise anything."

Aqua satin disappeared behind a pink curtain hanging from a shiny brass rod. Pursed-mouth looked at me, stretched her lips in a smile and moved a step closer. "Can I help you?"

"I hope so. I'm trying to find a young woman I was standing next to in a department store yesterday. We were both waiting at a counter. She took off her sunglasses and put them in her bag, and I took off *my* sunglasses and put them on the counter. The saleswoman came and I made my purchase, I was late for an appointment and rushed out of the store and didn't realize I'd left the glasses until I was in the car. When I went back to the counter, no one could find the glasses, and the young woman was gone. I thought she might have picked them up by mistake, but I had no way of finding her. Then, just now, I was passing your shop and remembered hearing her tell the saleswoman she was on the way to pick up her bridal gown because she was getting married on Saturday. I thought

155

perhaps you might know her. The glasses were prescription, you see."

Pursed-lips had her head tilted to one side, brow furrowed in polite attentiveness. "Saturday," she said. "Lynette?"

I caught myself before the "Yes!" escaped me. "A tall, dark-haired girl."

She nodded. "Lynette. She's going to make a lovely bride. White lace over peau de soie. The mother's is peach taffeta, with shoes dyed to match. Poor thing, I hope her feet are better, they were so swollen she couldn't get into the shoes. Nerves, of course. I see it all the time."

"Could you tell me where I could get in touch with—um—Lynette?"

"Byrnes. The last name is Byrnes. Until Saturday, of course. Grove Street, I think. Let me check." She trotted to a tiny white desk, consulted an appointments calendar bound in white leather, and confirmed the address. I thanked her and left the happily-ever-after shop, where white-and-gold-and-salmon-pink marriages were summoned forth in the blast of a punk rock world and the ghostly revving of B52 engines from the neighborhood apocalypse station.

No. 17 Grove Street was another box, but with individual touches. Weathered shingle instead of the prevailing stucco. A recessed wing added on one side, with two walls of continuous windows letting the outside world in, an anomaly in the guarded architecture of Padua. The windows overlooked not the usual elm or chestnut but a low-branched spreading apple tree, and the surrounding greenery, unmanicured, suggested a kind of country cottage. Odd. As I remembered Connie-with-the-knit-suit-and-pearls at the Sycamore, I would have expected small pruned borders on the outside, and all that went with it. An interior, I would think, full of Furniture-Heaven French Provincial. All the kitchen objects named: shakers called *Salt* and *Pepper,* a holder that said *Napkins,* a plastic cover emblazoned with *Toaster,* all for the benefit

156

of those inevitable visitors from another planet. There must be someone else's hand in this.

The garage door was open on a carless garage, garden tools and shovels hanging on the wall, a lawnmower stowed in the corner. But there was a familiar white Chevy in the driveway. Luck, finally, was with me. As I walked up the path to the front door a lawnmower started up in an adjoining yard, a mobile boiler factory rending the quiet of the suburban street.

No bell at the door, but a brass knocker in the shape of a shield, with the name Byrnes stamped in black letters. I knocked and waited. And knocked again and waited. No one came. I looked at the Chevy. With that sitting there, where could they be? Driven off in the Byrneses' car? But I remembered the bride-to-be complaining at the gas station the day before that Daddy worked odd hours and monopolized the car during the day. Was it possible the knock couldn't be heard over the racket of the power mower? Unlikely, if they were in the house. But they could be in the garden, yard, whatever it was they had back there. Drinks on the pah-tee-oh. 'Cause it's June, June, June . . .

I went around the side of the house, dandelions dotting the grass, lilacs growing against the side wall. Before I could turn the far corner into the backyard, the mower sputtered, stopped, and I heard the low, anguished cry.

"*Hit* me! He *hit* me!" And wrenching sobs.

"Connie—" It was Ethel Sprague's unmistakable voice: rubbing alcohol on the rocks. "Connie, stop it. You know Frank would never hit a woman."

"He *did!*"

"Did what, exactly?"

More sobbing, and then, between spasmodic gulps and swallows, "Came home . . . last night . . . this morning . . . two o'clock . . . I was sleeping . . . woke me up . . . in a rage . . . white . . . his face was white . . . I never saw him *look* like that . . ." More sobbing.

"Come on now, Connie."

The sobs subsided to gulps. "I was dreaming . . . that somebody was shaking me and yelling at me . . . but it was Frank . . ." The voice went thin and strangled. "I thought it was another nightmare . . . so many nightmares . . . for a week now . . . I had to take one of my pills . . . to sleep . . . and I was finally sleeping . . . and then he dragged me . . . dragged me out of bed . . . *cursing*. I . . . *hate* that kind of language . . . he . . . called . . . me . . ." Sobs, deep, desolate, hopeless.

"Connie, I can't help you if I don't know what happened. Now pull yourself together!"

A minute or so gulped by and finally: "He was screaming . . . 'out of my pockets!' . . . 'going through *my pockets!*' . . . 'keep your f . . . f . . . *hands* . . . out of my . . . pockets!' and . . . he . . . *hit* me . . . across . . . the *face!*"

From behind me the power mower ground its gears, screeched, started up again. I went back to the front of the house. Luck was not with me after all, merely teasing. There was no way I could interrupt this *cri de coeur*. I wouldn't get to utter a word before the boot landed.

Back in the car I debated whether or not to wait and catch Ethel Sprague as she left. Given Connie's state of acute misery, Ethel could very well be there the rest of the afternoon. It was two o'clock. Greenfield should be back at the Plaza shortly. I'd eaten nothing but crackers since the previous night. An investigative army travels on its stomach. I wouldn't need more than an hour to get to the Plaza, swallow a sandwich, report on progress and get back. I sat there for a while, looking at the quiet little house from which a daughter was about to be married off, in which a man had torn his wife from her bed in the night and ripped open a carefully stitched marriage, revealing old and ugly wounds.

Finally I turned the key in the ignition and pulled away from the curb to make a turn via the next driveway and head back to the boulevard. A hulking white sanitation truck lumbered up the middle of the road toward me. I waited for it to move to the side, and while one of the men was hauling trash from the curb, began to pass it, when the front door of no. 17 Grove Street opened and Ethel Sprague emerged, holding Connie's arm, leading her, crumpled, clutching her bag and dabbing at her eyes, down the path to the driveway. I stopped beyond the big truck and looked back. They were getting into the Chevy. To drive off in which direction? Ethel backed out of the driveway and took off, away from me, toward the boulevard. I pulled into the adjacent driveway, backed, turned, and the truck was once again in the middle of the road, impassable, blocking my view of the street ahead. It continued, at a speed of 2 mph, to the next clutch of curbside cans, then slowly moved to the side. By the time I got past it the Chevy was gone.

At the next corner I looked up and down the cross street, but there was no sign of it. No omen appeared to guide me, no vapor trail, no metaphysical glow or flash to right or left; they could have gone either way. They could be on their way to a doctor, a hospital, a marriage counselor, the airport, anywhere. I turned toward the center of town, zigzagged my way to the boulevard, and drove past the only two addresses with which Ethel had any permanent connection. There was no white Chevy parked near the stationery store, and none at the house on Westover. I ground my teeth and made for the Plaza.

CHAPTER FOURTEEN

GREENFIELD WAS NOT IN THE BAR, NOT IN THE dining room and not in number nine. I went back to the bar to wait. There was a game show in progress on the box, tuned mercifully low. Julius was busy serving beer to two young men, and I recognized Brenda's Michael and his sidekick, looking hot, unshaven and weary, arguing about something.

"You lost it, you lost it, you had a belt full of dead batteries!" Michael held the cold glass against his forehead.

"It wasn't the batteries. I *told* you I was getting an intermittent signal, it's the goddamn cable connection, people walking all over the goddamn cable, what do you expect?"

"Then you get that backup cable hooked up *today*. And recharge the batteries anyway."

Julius came over and gave me a ginger ale. I dug in my bag and he put a hand gently on my wrist. "On the house."

I smiled at him. Not exactly Greenfield's charismatic lieutenant colonel, but we gather rosebuds where we may. I'd taken two sips of the ginger ale when Michael moved down the bar and took the stool next to mine.

"You're Brenda's friend, right? From the camp?"

I nodded.

"The one who met Alice Dakin, before she disappeared."

For a moment I wondered if he knew she'd been found, but no, if he had, he'd be running around photographing the stream, the police, the morgue. "I wouldn't say I'd met her. I went to a fifteen-minute briefing where she spoke to the press."

"Look, I'm filming a documentary on the women's protest. How would you—"

"Here's Mr. Greenfield," Julius said.

I looked over my shoulder. Greenfield was standing in the doorway. He moved his head fractionally as a suggestion that I join him.

I smiled an apology at Michael. "Sorry, I have an appointment."

In the hallway Greenfield was staring at the wood paneling with unseeing eyes. Thinking, he was.

"I have to eat," I said.

He nodded. "They have food at the Sycamore Inn. I want to see the Dakin staff."

The only time I'd driven to the Sycamore was with Brenda, and then from another direction. I took a street that should, by all the laws of geography, have led to the Sycamore. It didn't, because it made a loop, as unfamiliar streets so often do. A lone pedestrian eventually put an end to my floundering. Greenfield was largely oblivious to all this: in the car he'd found Wednesday's edition of the *Ledger* on the passenger seat, spent the trip reading it

161

exhaustively, and put it aside only when we climbed the small hill, drove past the flower beds and parked opposite the pseudo-Greek façade of the motel.

Looking up, Greenfield's casual glance was arrested by the mock-Ionic columns. He gazed at them in wonder.

"Athens," he observed, "gives birth to the House of Pancakes."

At the front desk, Greenfield was told that all the Dakin people were temporarily absent. The news must have reached them, he decided. They were down at the morgue, identifying, asking questions, getting no answers. We went to the dining room. Tomato omelettes, rather good, and melon, and coffee, and almost-hot rolls.

I said, "What were you looking for in the *Ledger?*"

He gave me an answer, but it was a long time coming. He began by telling me he'd been given the grand tour of the base on the most superficial level, seen the bowling lanes, the Olympic-size swimming pool, the recreation hall, the convenience store, the string of pretty commanders' houses, the enlisted men's barracks, the exterior of the regional operations control center that monitored airspace for unidentified aircraft and scrambled the fighters in case of an alert, the research center, the Alert Barn where the fighter squadron took turns at twenty-four-hour periods of wakeful readiness, the B52s, the runway. And, only because he was a friend of the lieutenant colonel's uncle, the house—exterior—of the commander and wife who had entertained Alice Dakin the night of her disappearance.

"There was an event going on, the night that Dakin disappeared," he said, "in the recreation hall. A bowling competition, teams from both the base personnel and the local civilians: the base obviously making an effort to maintain good relations with the town. The public was invited." He let that sink in, then added, "The front of the commander's house is within clear sight of the entrance to the recreation hall." And paused, gently buttering the remains of a roll. "I asked my host if the event had been covered by the local press. He said, 'The media'—I'm

162

quoting him—'are always encouraged to cover these things.' " Finally he'd arrived at the answer to my question. "Wednesday's *Ledger* devotes the space to a recounting of the scores and there's only one picture, of two airmen, one of them watching the other make a strike."

"What were you hoping for?"

He looked at his coffee. "Unreasonable luck. Something to confound the laws of probability. A shot of a group of people coming out of the recreation hall at ten-twenty-five that night and among them someone recognizable, someone who appears frequently in the *Ledger*'s daily cuts of the scene at the entrance to the base: the man we saw waving the American flag, or the woman you were going to track down." He looked up. "Did you find her?"

I have difficulty admitting failure. I postponed it. "Why did the abductor have to be at the recreation hall?"

"I didn't say he had to, only that if he was, then he—or she—might have been photographed. In any case, he or she had to have been on the base."

"Either legally," I said pointedly, "or illegally."

He closed his eyes briefly. "Stop pushing that theory, Maggie. I've rejected it. And if you're postulating some other lawbreaker, it's highly unlikely, for a number of reasons. The abductor was on the base legally. And probably without a car of his or her own."

"Because—?"

"Because technology has yet to come up with a way for one person to drive two cars simultaneously. Dakin's car was found near Hunegger. Presumably the abductor was in the car with her. If he'd driven his own car onto the base, he'd have to leave it there and come back for it, in which case he'd have to risk showing his pass to get back in, or sneak back onto the base and risk being seen doing it."

"Or he could have had a car parked outside the base, waiting," I said, still thinking of The Five.

"And walked back from Hunegger to get back to it? That would narrow the field. We'd only have to look for someone who's been getting around in a wheelchair since Tuesday."

Something tickled my mind and disappeared. "He might have had a confederate," I insisted, partly with H.-M. on my mind, partly because once you enter the game you have to play it. "A confederate who either drove his car off the base or had it waiting at a designated spot."

"Yes, he might. He might also have had roller skates, a bicycle, or a sleigh with eight reindeer—that's not really the vital aspect of the theory. The vital one is that he had to be on the base, because the alternative is that Dakin drove off the base alone and picked up someone on the outside. And I find it impossible to convince myself that a woman of her temperament would stop, at night, in a strange town, and pick up anyone."

"Unless it was someone she knew. Someone she had arranged to meet. Secretly. A double agent."

"You're wasting your time working for me, you could be making a fortune with Rupert Murdoch."

"Come to think of it, if you're looking for the abductor among people who are hostile to the camp, there are eight thousand of them living on that base. In Air Force uniform."

He sighed. "Don't bother with Murdoch. You're in Tolkien territory." He drained his cup. "Now that we've exhausted the red herring, would you mind telling me whether or not you found that woman you were supposed to be questioning?"

I scraped at my melon. I swallowed some coffee. Finally I gave him the sequence of events, in all their exquisite detail.

He leaned back and regarded the flower beds beyond the dining room window as though the red and purple petunias were deliberately obstructing our progress. He sat for so long, in a kind of bilious trance, that my thoughts flowed off in another direction, down the deeply dug channel that led to Heath-Morecomb. Not only did I want to drop Greenfield's needle-in-a-haystack nonsense, I wanted to drop it all. I had no desire to bring anyone to what passes for justice. I wanted no part of the inevitable discovery that those five women at the camp were responsible for that body in the stream. My only impulse had been to avert disaster. Abduction might have been reversible: *extinction* was not. So far as I knew. And if those women *weren't* responsible, why had JoAnne gone to see that doctor, what had Harriet shoved into the desk drawer so quickly, where had Heath-Morecomb gone when she reached the stream? The whole business had become appalling. Horrendous. Didn't bear thinking about.

"The *media,*" Greenfield mused. "I suppose that means television. One of those local newscasts. Twenty-five-year-olds with cameras strapped to their shoulders and dreams of the anchor desk in their hearts."

Michael, I thought, with the fringe of my mind. And "Michael" I must have said aloud.

"Michael? What Michael?"

I suddenly felt tired. The onslaught of food after such long abstinence had affected me like a sedative. "There's a girl"—I yawned—"at the camp. You saw her with me at the Plaza. Brenda. She has—um—struck up an acquaintance with a young man who's filming a documentary of the protest. She said, Brenda said—of course, she's addicted to hyperbole so I don't know how factual this is" —yawn—"her exact words were—'Michael spends all day taking pictures, and then at night he goes on the base and takes more pictures.' But even if it's true, I don't know why he'd want to shoot a bowling tournament."

Greenfield thought about it. "Might he have known Dakin was going to be on the base that night?"

"I doubt," I said wearily, "there's been a syllable spoken in Padua that he hasn't recorded. Not a potato chip crunched that isn't on tape. You think he used the bowling thing as a cover to get some footage of her?"

"See if you can find him."

I blinked my closing eyes at him. "He was right there

165

at the bar in the Plaza. I was talking to him when you showed up."

"Call Julius."

I somnambulated to the lobby. Michael, of course, was gone. There'd most likely been a newscast in the interim. I told Greenfield he was probably busy chasing after the corpse, or the Dakin staff, or taking random reaction shots.

"Go after him."

I blinked. "He might show up here."

"I'll hold on to him if he does."

Michael, I thought blearily, driving I knew not where. Where would Michael go first? Could he have been on the base Tuesday night? Would "media" red carpet extend to a free-lance documentary-maker? Would Michael have faked some ID to get in? Did he have his sights on Dakin? Had he . . . seen anything? *Is that how he'd learned, so early, that she was missing? Did he merely have a news-hound's lucky nose? Or was he—possibly—ambitious to the point of staging the drama himself?*

Was Michael—himself—suspect?

Idiot. Michael had been at the Plaza, at ten on Tuesday night.

The Honda apparently wanted to go to the camp. It drove itself up to the grounds, past the information booth and up the track to a parking area that had disappeared under an ocean of metal. Cars, vans, motorcycles, a pickup truck, a fleet of bicycles, one trailer . . . and an ambulance. St. Vincent's Hospital, its back doors standing open. An ambulance!

No place to park. The grounds looked alien, propor-tions rearranged, landmarks lost under a human bee-swarm. Legs, arms, heads moved incessantly over the grass. A constant hum, as though the place were running on electric current, the very meadows wired to some giant generator: more marchers for Saturday, their numbers growing hourly.

I drove onto the forbidden rough grass of the first camping area, left the car, ran to the barn, catching sight of a familiar face here and there, like a buoy bobbing up among whitecaps. I pushed through the crowded little outer room —no Doris there—down the length of the crowded main working barn: JoAnne, her face pale and set, making way for two white-coated men carrying a stretcher.

Harriet lying on it. Waxen. Eyes closed, mouth open. I turned, frantic for explanation, and saw Brenda.

"*What?*" I demanded.

She pulled me into the office. "Heart attack," she said. "I think it's probably minor. She got onto the stretcher kind of by herself. My uncle had a massive one and he didn't look like that, he looked like a whale with six hundred harpoons in him. She's been working like a nut, Harriet, she didn't want anybody to know she had a problem, in case they made her go home. I think JoAnne knew, but you know JoAnne, she's probably got a great-grandmother who drove a whole wagon train to Wyoming or somewhere, those women can still shoot a rifle when they're ninety-seven, they don't believe in sickness."

I exhaled for a while. "I think JoAnne believed. I think she was probably worried enough to go see a doctor about Harriet."

"Yeah?" She looked at me. "Where've you been?"

"Busy. Would you stand at the door and let me know if anyone looks as though they're heading in here?" Brenda screwed up her eyes at me, but went to the door. I moved behind the desk and opened the top right-hand drawer. A stack of bills held together with a large paper clip: Clayton Roofing, Pierce Brothers Plumbing, Hunegger Hardware. A box of Kleenex. A stapler. A small brown bottle, Arvine Drugs, prescription label pasted on, undecipherable. The bottle contained only a half-dozen tiny white tablets. I closed the drawer. "Dakin's been found," I said.

She turned and lowered her head at me, like a bull getting ready for a defensive toss. "You're kidding."

"In the stream. She's dead."

Her mouth opened wide, then closed enough to say, "No shit."

"I think Michael heard about it and took off with the camera. He was at the Plaza, and then he disappeared. You haven't seen him in the last hour?"

"I *did,* he drove me here from the gate, he didn't say a word!"

"I'm wrong, then, I thought he'd caught the newscast. Do you know where he went?"

"Somewhere to work on the equipment. They were having trouble with their cable. Tell me about Dakin!"

"You mean a repair shop? Where would they go in Padua to fix a cable?"

"I only know what's in Manhattan, and in Manhattan I only know locksmiths. They were going back to where they stay, I think. To the trailer camp. Why?"

"Where's the trailer camp?"

"Listen, what's going on, what do you want with Michael? Something weird's going on, right?"

"Right. You take me to the trailer camp and I'll tell you all about it." Some of it, at any rate.

"How can I take you, I've never been there. I told you, he's a lost cause."

I began to sink into Harriet's chair, and stopped myself. Somehow it didn't seem the thing to do. "You have no idea where it is?" I checked the mail slots for a message from Elliot. Nothing.

"I told you. A trailer camp, is all I know."

Some cranial synapse passed things along from neuron to neuron and I remembered the wide yellow trailer trundling down the dirt road.

West Crannock. Oh God. Fifteen tortuous miles each way.

Brenda insisted on accompanying me, even though I explained that it would be like driving from the Battery to the Bronx on nothing but one-way streets going the wrong way. For forty minutes we drove, while I divided my concentration between retracing a hazily remembered route and fielding the questions my story of Dakin elicited from Brenda.

A few miles short of West Crannock, a dirt road appeared on the left. I tried to visualize the wide yellow trailer waddling down it: yes, it had that disturbing quality of a scene faintly recalled. I turned into the dirt road and followed it through encroaching trees and bushes to where it opened into a cleared three-acre patch, dotted with trailers, big, small and mega-sized, with names like Leisuretime and Carcottage, hoses like umbilical cords attaching them to the electric water outlets. Some had an awning stretched out from one side, under which a selection of folding chairs awaited tired bottoms, some had geraniums growing warily in pots standing on the natural gas tanks, some a pup tent pegged to the ground nearby for the kids. On a picnic table, her bare feet resting on the bench, a woman sat peeling potatoes. And between a dirty white Sunfun and a lavish Openroad the size of a double-decker bus we found Michael's bright red van. The two men were sitting on bedrolls in the flat roomy space behind the front seats, black cable snaking over the floor among the video equipment. Michael was taken aback at sight of us. "What's up?"

Brenda looked at me. I'd threatened her with mayhem if she mentioned the body in the stream before I accomplished what I'd come for.

"It's possible, Michael," I said, "that you have some footage in your tapes that's worth a lot of money. Assuming you were on the base Tuesday night."

He laughed uneasily. "You want to be a little more specific?"

"It occurred to me that if you were there, for instance, taking shots of the people at the bowling event, those shots might include the face of the person responsible for Dakin's disappearance."

He looked at the other young man, who stared at him owlishly, then back at me. "You're kidding. Would you recognize him?"

"I might."

"How?"

"No point going into that unless you were there."

The two men stared at each other again. Brenda, ambiguously, said, "Michael, let her look at the tapes, it could turn out to be the most important thing you ever did."

Michael stared at the wall of the van, where, presumably, the carrot was being dangled.

His assistant said, "Mike, so what, we were there."

Michael shut his eyes and looked pained. "Barry, for Christ's sake—"

Wondering if I was being shrewd or incredibly foolish, I said, "Brenda, didn't you tell him we were arrested Tuesday night?"

"Thanks a lot," she said. "Could I run my own life now?"

"Arrested?" Michael's eyes were alive with documentary greed.

"You weren't the only one," I assured him, pressing home the point, "who was on the base illegally. I'm sure we all know how to keep quiet."

That did it. After a great deal of sorting through tapes and fiddling with the camera, Michael finally draped my shoulder with a Port-a-Pack like a millstone on a shoulder brace, and showed me how to clutch the handle and look into the eyepiece.

"This isn't the ideal way to see it," he said, "but we're having trouble with the monitor. The only filmmakers in the entire Northeast with *two* damaged cables. Also, you won't have any sound. Here, can you see anything? Okay. Now you're probably going to lose something at the very end, because I forgot to stop short of the tail. The last minute on a cassette is biased electronically and the image can go screwy."

"That's all right," I said desperately, feeling like Atlas with the world slipped to one side. "Let's just—um—roll it."

For the first few minutes I seemed to be looking at grass growing, at water moving through a pipe, at fireflies in slow motion. Then the images sorted themselves out and I saw the no-frills façade of a functional building, a number of uniforms, back views of several broad-beamed women in slacks, a few self-conscious middle-aged men exchanging hearty remarks in neat short-sleeved shirts, a pair of bare female arms, hands clutching a white leather bag, faces laughing, faces alert, faces shy, faces cocky, leaden, grave and playful, secretive and on parade. None of the faces belonged to Ethel Sprague. None belonged to the man who'd been waving the American flag. Except for one innocuous face that I'd seen elsewhere, none seemed familiar for having seen it, hostile or otherwise, at the gate.

CHAPTER FIFTEEN

THE DAY HAD TURNED CLOUDY IN LATE AFTER-
noon, and now with the light fading from a doleful gray
blanket of sky, it was not so much raining as gently mist-
ing. It was as though all of us, animal and mineral as well
as vegetable, were so many plants in a nursery, being
carefully watered by a fine automatic spray.

As it turned out, the English weather was appropriate.
I found Greenfield at a table in the Plaza bar. I found
Heath-Morecomb with him.

They had drinks on the table before them, and she, dark
copper filaments of hair corkscrewing over the avocado
green of her shirt, was leaning forward over the table,
emphasizing a conversational point with a brandished
pretzel stick. Greenfield watched her with that quiet, ap-
preciative stillness that makes a gift of diamonds tawdry

by comparison. I stood in the doorway forcing myself not to turn and leave. Dakin was dead, Harriet was on the brink, and H.-M. was having drinks in the bar, back at the old spellbinding stand.

Julius saw me, beamed, brought forth a bottle of ginger ale, and I started for the long mahogany counter, but Greenfield's voice, pitched low, reached me. Without taking his eyes from her, he said, "Maggie. Join us." His peripheral vision was average: his psychic antenna remarkable. I went to the table. Heath-Morecomb gave me a quick smile without interrupting her monologue.

"You can*not* be neutral in this, Charlie," she was saying, "and I most certainly will not allow you to be patronizing. *I* don't know what's to be done about the nuclear arsenal once it's been disassembled or whatever needs doing. If the half-life of the uranium or the neutrons or any of the components is twenty billion years, then the people who *opened* this bloody Pandora's box are damned well going to have to shut it. My *God,* I find the scientific mind horrendous. All those brains and not a moral imperative between them. The point is, you don't sit back with the bomb in your lap because the problem of how to bury it takes a bit of thought. Fussing with the federal deficit, for *God's* sake, while the world's hanging by a thread!" She bit off the top of the pretzel stick.

Greenfield dropped his eyes from her face to his drink, and lifted the glass. "I've noticed the word 'patronizing' generally crops up whenever I question someone's grasp of reality. You . . . plural . . ."—he sipped the drink—"are expecting the political colossi of the world to be moved because your hearts are pure and your cause is **just:** purity and justice are defined differently in the lexicons of the decision-makers. They have been singularly schooled, uniquely indoctrinated. They perceive life through a blemished prism. *They*—are the problem. And that's a simplification. In any case, the scientists are only company employees. The nuclear arsenal is only their product. What has to be dealt with is not only something made from particles of uranium, but something fashioned in the cells that combine to form a human brain; the deformed mental process, the perverted list of priorities, the grotesque sense of values.

"Until you've changed those attributes, you're merely making gestures. Dispose of nuclear weapons, and while you're doing it they will already be replacing them with something beyond the unthinkable. The first rule of battle is to point your guns at the enemy, not at the shadow he casts."

Heath-Morecomb threw her hands in the air. "I've been impaled!"

Had she, indeed.

She gave him a wry smile. "You're right, of course, but you haven't bested me for all that. *Je suis contre!* We must first survive long enough, Charlie, to get the target in our sights."

That was twice she'd used his first name. I bit the rim of the glass of ginger ale Julius had brought me.

Greenfield turned to me. "A productive afternoon?"

"I'm not sure. And you?"

"It's been quiet."

Heath-Morecomb tipped her glass and drank. "I haven't seen you for days, Maggie. You know Alice Dakin's been found."

"Yes, I know."

"You'll hear no sad songs from me on that account, but of course it will be a bloody mess for the camp. Someone tried to incriminate me—" For a moment something raw showed in her face, like a lance wound seen through a rent in the chain mail, then it was gone. "And that will no doubt keep the law on our doorstep for a while, gumming up the works. It was too much for Harriet, she's in hospital, the coronary arteries rebelled. She's *very* brave, poor, foolish Harriet."

Foolish Harriet. Wouldn't be left out of your vanity plot, no matter what the cost.

"I drove Brenda back to the camp just now," I said

grudgingly. "Doris said the hospital bulletin was that Harriet's condition is stable." A report that never failed to fill me with anxiety.

She turned her mercurial eyes on me for a probing moment, ran a hand through the brightness of her hair, reached down beside the chair and stood up, holding her violin case. "I must get over to the gate." She looked at me. "Are you going that way? I didn't bring my car."

I looked at Greenfield. He pushed his chair back. "I brought you here. I'll take you back. You'd better come with us, Maggie. I found my way there by luck, and fortunately had guidance on the return trip."

He could find his way to a specific rock in the mountains of Tibet if need be; the invitation had nothing to do with guidance. We piled into the Plymouth, me in the back seat like a mother-in-law. To be Greenfield's mother-in-law, I thought, I would need an instant access of at least thirty years.

No new moisture on the windshield, I noticed, once he'd used the wipers: the mist had been suspended. Heath-Morecomb was uncharacteristically pensive, only a few desultory remarks about Padua as we covered the distance. At the gate she gave Greenfield a final, odd, regretful smile, flicked a hand in my direction and strode away through the group of protesters, carrying the violin case like a lunch box.

Greenfield turned into the next side street and parked.

"What did you find?" he asked.

"I found Michael. I had to do a little horse-trading but he finally admitted to being on the base Tuesday night. He had tape on it, but I didn't see any shots of Ethel Sprague, only that friend of hers. It's possible I've seen some of those other faces, but unless a passing adversary actually looks like William F. Buckley I'm not likely to remember. The only way we can do it, Charlie, is to go through the cuts from the *Ledger* and mark any faces that appear often enough to signify, and then have those photographs beside us while we're running the tape. And even then we'd each need four eyes."

He looked back toward the gate.

"Why are we sitting here?" I inquired. "Why didn't I just wait for you at the Plaza?"

"We're here because I have bottomless faith in you."

"That's lovely but a little obscure."

"I sent you to find Michael. I naturally assumed you found him and saw the tape." He got out of the car, opened the back door, "And that having the tape relatively fresh in your mind, you might look over the crowd here and see if you recognize anyone."

I got out and we walked back. "What happened at the Sycamore?"

"The Dakin crew," he said, "arrived at the Sycamore like lost sheep. They were inarticulate and disoriented. Bleating inanely. They'd lost their shepherd. The only piece of coherent information I garnered was the fact that Dakin disliked being a passenger when she was going anywhere by car. 'She always had to be in the driver's seat,' was the way one girl put it. That, I suppose, would explain why she drove herself to the base, instead of being chauffeured by staff or by host." His eyes raked the group of local inhabitants who stood watching the activity at the gate. It was dinnertime, the numbers of both watchers and chanters somewhat depleted by the need to feed. Heath-Morecomb, violin in hand, was talking, with a directorial air, to two women from the camp, one of whom held a flute, the other a guitar. She waved her bow at the chanters, who fell silent, tucked the violin under her chin, nodded to the instrumentalists, and began to play, of all things, the melody of *Sheep May Safely Graze,* while the flute and guitar supplied the harmonic base. Where had she found the time to teach them that?

"A Bach cantata," Greenfield murmured. "Formidable woman."

Words came swimming hazily out of memory. *If the sovereign wisely ruleth, ever peace and plenty floweth, and*

176

the land reward doth reap. I was impressed. So, apparently, were the onlookers, so were the guards behind the fence. All eyes, for the moment, were on the trio. H.-M. had taken her usual position facing the fence. She stood opposite the big security guard, the one who'd handcuffed Brenda and me on the base, the one I'd seen that first night, watching H.-M. so carefully. I glanced away, and then quickly back again.

That guard's face of his that I remembered as so detached, so unreadable, with that faint hint of secret amusement, had been laid bare, stripped of its impassivity, ripped open. Torment had clawed deep channels from eye to mouth, pain shouted silently from every line: the strong man as victim, caught in the unimaginable position of being flayed alive. I gaped.

"Makes strong men weep," she'd said. Could music be doing all that?

I turned to Greenfield. He was staring, transfixed, at the scene, in something like surprise. Or foreboding.

I tapped his arm. "What's wrong?"

He shrugged and looked back at the townspeople. "What do you see?"

"Sorry. I was distracted." I looked them over now, several times, and shook my head. "Nobody."

He led me from the gate. Walking back to the car, he said, "One way and another I've had a day full of sheep." He was silent after that, the kind of Greenfield silence that announced he was beyond reach of a human voice. Then, his hand on the car door, he suddenly said, "On the tape, you say you recognized a friend of Ethel Sprague's? What friend?"

"The one I told you about at lunch, the one who was crying in her backyard. She was at the bowling thing, I suppose, looking a little glum, carrying that handbag of hers. For whatever that's worth."

We got into the Plymouth. Greenfield sat behind the wheel for a while, staring through the windshield at the quiet, dusk-shadowed street.

"How do I get to this woman's house? The one you saw on the tape?"

I didn't ask why, it was more than likely he didn't really know. Lack of anything else to do, most likely. I directed him to the boulevard, north to a street I remembered with a narrow little church on the corner, west again, and north, and west, and there we were at 17 Grove Street. The house was dark, not a light in any of the windows. Garage door shut, no car inside.

"She went off with Ethel," I said, "and maybe even home to mother." We were standing in the driveway.

Greenfield looked at the house, at the lawn, at the shrubs and the apple tree. "Wherever she went," he said, "she'll have to surface in the next day or so if her daughter's getting married." He went up the walk to the front door, peered through a window, lifted the door knocker and lowered it again noiselessly.

A man came out of the house next door. "You looking for someone?"

After sundown, the neighborhood watch.

"Chuzzlewit," Greenfield replied, "Martin Chuzzlewit."

"No one by that name on this street."

We drove back to the Plaza, and before leaving the Plymouth, I leaned over and retrieved my poplin jacket from the back seat—my protection against the mist, picked up when I'd dropped Brenda at the camp. Pulling it over the seat, something fell out of the pocket and clattered to the floor at my feet. It was the cassette I'd found on the second floor of the burned-out house at the camp. I picked it up, remembering the smoke I'd smelled in that room.

"Oh yes," I said, "a little something I found in a strange place."

I gave it to him and told him its provenance.

"You think it's hers?" He read the name on the label. "Bizet. Why did you keep it?"

"I haven't worn the jacket since then. I forgot I had it."

178

They coined the word "skeptical" for just the kind of glance he gave me. It's truth that inspires mistrust. I've lied so many times with impunity. He turned the cassette, slowly, over and over in his hand, then gave it back. We left the car in the lot, went into the hotel, took a table in the dining room, and ordered veal Milanese and a bottle of house wine. Greenfield ate abstractedly, staring at his fork for long seconds before remembering why he was holding it. I cut off a button-size piece of veal and chewed it without enthusiasm. A late lunch and now this. Feast or famine. Finally Greenfield said, "You never heard any mention of the husband before today?"

"Connie's husband? Nothing much. Just that he was behaving moodily, according to his daughter. That he doesn't go to work in the morning like ordinary fathers."

"No hint of what he does to earn the daily bread? Where he works?"

"No. Why?"

"You could probably find out from Ethel Sprague, if she's done playing nursemaid."

"You can't be serious. After that woman has spent the afternoon binding the wounds inflicted by a man called Byrnes, a strange female knocks on the door, in a patently suspect guise, and in the course of some obviously contrived research, just happens to ask a few pointed questions about the very same Byrnes? Lights would flash. Sirens would go off."

"You're not that clumsy and she's probably not that perceptive. I don't see any other way to get the information."

"Ask Julius. He knows everyone in this town. Or so he said."

He looked up. "What made him say that?"

"The first time he saw me, he said, 'How are things at the camp?' I asked him what made him think I was from the camp, and he said his family had owned this hotel for sixty-three years, and if I lived here, he'd know me."

Greenfield ate a veal medallion without being aware of it.

"Why've you latched onto the husband?" I asked.

"I'm thinking," he muttered.

He spent the rest of the meal alone. I was there beside him, swallowing bits of mushrooms, shreds of salad, other diners talked and laughed, the waitress came and went, but there was no one around, where he was. Alone, pursuing some elusive answer down the twisting paths of an inner landscape.

Then, suddenly, a question. "You mentioned there was a picture of her in one of those clippings from the *Ledger*'s daily coverage."

"Who?"

A pause while he summoned patience. "Eleanor Roosevelt."

"Well, Charlie, the last time we spoke we mentioned several people and then you took a trip to some desert island—"

"The woman," he said quietly, "whose house we just visited. I wouldn't recognize her picture. See if you can find it." He handed me the room key.

I drained my wineglass, went up to room number nine, found two pictures of Connie, at the gate, one taken the previous Friday night, one the Wednesday before that, and brought them down. He studied them without comment, folded them, put them in his pocket and contemplated the tablecloth for a while. I was beginning to regret not having brought along something to read.

"Julius," he said eventually, "seems to find you sympathetic. You might try sounding him out about his family."

Julius's family? I was lost. The brain gave up the battle. An overload, I could hear the cerebral repair man say, it's only a machine, you know, you can't push in all that unrelated stuff and not expect some jamming.

"Now?" I said. "What would I be doing in the bar *now*? How could I justify it?"

"Have a drink."

"I've just drunk. I've just eaten."

"Julius doesn't know that."

"Julius"—I got up—"is going to put us down as barflies."

"Julius does not judge. He puts the money in the till."

"He'll notice when I don't drink what I order."

"Spill it."

The waitress went by, a shy, plain-faced girl with heavy dark eyebrows and hair that just hung, and Greenfield stopped her and asked for more coffee and the check. I went into the bar, where silly music was coming from the radio and Julius was arranging glasses. Sliding onto a stool, I waited for him to look up, and when he did, gave him a wistful smile. He gave back a cheerful one.

"Ginger ale?"

"I'll have some sherry, Julius." He brought the sherry. I raised the glass. "Here's to a better day tomorrow."

"You had a bad day today?"

"Sort of. I'm a little worried about one of my boys. Nothing serious, but . . . if you have children, you know what I mean."

He shrugged. "It all works out. How many've you got?"

"Two. How about you?"

"Four girls. Three of them have babies. I'm a grandpa three times." He brought forth pictures: round cheeks, black hair, shoe-button eyes. I admired them lavishly. The young mother of one of the infants looked faintly familiar.

I gave them back. "Which one do you think will be running the hotel when you retire?"

He chuckled. "Who knows? Maybe none of them."

"You wouldn't let the Plaza go to someone outside the family? After sixty-three years?"

"You can't tell kids what to do. They move away."

"It would be such a shame." I looked around, sentimentally. "I believe in continuity."

"Well, who knows. Continuity. I suppose. Maybe somebody will. It's a big family."

"How many?"

He laughed. "Big! When we have a wedding, we need two churches!"

The word jolted me. I forced a smile, sipped my sherry. "With a family that big, you must be going to a wedding every other week."

Julius looked suddenly anxious and made a tepid joke. "That's what keeps me broke." He moved to the far end of the bar and fussed around, mopping up, removing glasses.

Greenfield wandered in, glanced unhappily toward the radio that was sending forth sounds he would ordinarily greet with *"Merde!"* and went to a distant table. I joined him.

"Does he have a family?" he asked.

"Extensive." I repeated the conversation, in an undertone, swirling the sherry in the glass.

He took the *Ledger* pictures from his pocket, put them on the table, and looked over at the bar, until he caught Julius's eye. Julius came trotting to the table, bearing goodwill as though on a tray, and Greenfield pulled over a third chair.

"Can you join us for a minute?"

"A minute, sure." He perched on the chair, hands on his knees, weight on his feet.

"I'm looking for someone who might be able to help me," he told Julius, "with an article I want to write for my paper. The person must have certain qualifications. I think I might find what I'm looking for among these people"— he pushed the two *Ledger* photographs toward Julius— "but I need identification. Name and occupation. Do you know any of them?"

Julius looked at the pictures. "Larraby," he said, pointing. "Insurance. Zwerlin, he's a jeweler. Coleccio, the family business is farm machinery. Not doing so good. That looks like Betty Hansen back there, she works in the mayor's office. . . ." He identified almost every face that could be seen clearly.

"What about these two?" Greenfield pointed to Ethel and Connie.

There was a tiny pause, a miniature freeze of the facial muscles. Julius looked up quickly, with an apologetic gesture. "Aw, dammit—excuse me—I forgot about the beer. Let me go take care of it, I'll be right back."

He didn't come back, he got very busy at the bar, stretched the five patrons into a hundred little tasks that needed urgent attention.

Julius? I thought incredulously. *Being evasive and inaccessible?* It was equivalent to a cherub slinking through a dark alley in a trench coat.

Greenfield stood up. "Let's find a public phone," he said, "that doesn't belong to Julius."

"In Padua, public phones don't exactly beckon from every street corner. Especially at this hour."

"Even in Spider Flats, Montana, there's a bus station that stays open past nine o'clock."

"I have no idea where the Padua bus station is."

"Maggie. You should be able to spend a week in the hinterlands without becoming literal-minded."

"You'll take that back at three A.M., when we end up at the bus station."

"September twenty-fourth, 1948," he said wryly, "was the last time I recanted."

There was always the Sycamore, of course, but I didn't relish trying to find it in the dark. As it happened, the streetlight in front of the gas station, when we drove by, revealed a booth near the curb at the far end. Greenfield combined the change in his pocket with the change in my bag.

"What country are you calling?" I asked.

"Xanadu," he said, and went to make his secret call while I waited in the Honda.

Xanadu. Really. Was that another bit of whimsy, like "Martin Chuzzlewit"; or did it mean something? The pleasure dome of Kubla Khan? I gave it up.

I saw him speak, hang up, stand there with the door slightly open until the phone rang, and speak again.

When he returned to the car, it was with a heavier step and a face tight with controlled apprehension, like a migraine victim who has recognized the first signal of approaching agony.

CHAPTER SIXTEEN

I SET THE WIPERS GOING AS WE DROVE THROUGH the thin, dark drizzle. The suspended mist had reconsidered and decided on commitment: real drops splashed against the windshield. I still had no clue to the nature of that phone call in the booth, and we were almost back at the hotel. Greenfield had answered my "What's happened?" with a cryptic "Nature, I'm afraid, may have taken its customary course," and devoted himself to gazing moodily at the rain.

There was always a point, in these enterprises, when Greenfield became allusive and enigmatic, and it meant communication was suspended until further notice. It was a nifty arrangement, a perfect partnership. All the information *I* gathered was our common property, and all the critical discoveries *he* made belonged to him exclusively. In days of yore it was called marriage.

He finally spoke, but not, of course, to the point. "Have you ever seen the back entrance to the Plaza?"

"It never occurred to me there was one."

"A back entrance has been a necessity for some time, in fable and in fact. The Trojan Horse had one. Elsinore had one. The Winter Palace at Saint Petersburg. The Colosseum. Front doors are for company, the back ones are where they let the lions in."

"I haven't seen a single lion at the Plaza."

"You were busy looking at the moldings. When we get there, I want to do a little exploring."

Silence.

"I just want you to know," I said, "that I hate this. I should refuse to do another thing until you tell me what you're thinking."

"You're free to do that."

"What do I gain? Investigative colossi are not moved by a pure heart and a just cause."

"You show promise," he murmured, "you're beginning to recognize limits." But the banter was halfhearted and his face was drawn. I wondered if he was coming down with a summer cold.

I turned into the small parking lot and pulled up next to a panel truck. Greenfield moved as though to leave, then changed his mind.

"I assume you noticed the resemblance," he said, "between Julius and that woman in the *Ledger* clippings?"

"I wouldn't have, but he showed me a picture of his daughter and she seemed familiar, reminded me of someone. Some casual fixture back home, I thought, a bank teller or someone similar. Then he mentioned weddings and I made the connection. She looks like Connie."

"Does the resemblance suggest anything to you?"

"Well, obviously, it suggests they're related. And Julius is trying to hide the connection, skulking around like a secret agent. Meaning what? Julius and his family are in the smuggling business? Illegal veal?"

He stared at the rain spattering on the glass, running downward in twisting rivulets to join with other rivulets. Minutes passed.

"Charlie—talk. I just want to hear your voice. Say anything. Quote a passage from Turgenev. Tell me again about Webern admitting that Stravinsky had some talent. Anything."

He drew breath from some abyss, and exhaled slowly. "It's all conjecture."

"I'll take it."

"I'm hypothesizing: the back door of the hotel opens into a room from which a stairway ascends to the upper floors."

"And—?"

He was quiet again. Then, "Extrapolate," he said, and opened the car door and loped through the drizzle toward the hotel. I went after him, into the amber-lit entrance hall and up the stairs. Straight ahead, room number nine was at the far end of the corridor where it turned sharply to the right and disappeared. To our left the corridor continued behind us. Greenfield made a U-turn at the top of the stairs and we followed the corridor back toward the rear of the building.

"Charlie, what did you—" He raised a hand like a stop sign and I clenched my teeth. *Someday* . . . At the end of the corridor we met a blank wall. No backstairs here. We turned and reversed down the corridor, past Greenfield's room, right turn to the end of that passage, and right again toward the back of the building. Here, opposite the door to room two, we found a narrow, uncarpeted stairway.

It occurred to me, as we made our way down in the dim light from a single wall sconce, that the kitchen help might still be around, though it was late for that. I visualized descending into a tableau of upturned faces as the backstairs crew stood around in stained aprons, stoking themselves with leftover veal, but there was a lone figure standing at a counter near an oversized stainless-steel sink, preparing a tray: coffee pot and a covered dish. It was the young dining room waitress with the lank hair. She looked at us, dumbstruck.

"Forgive the intrusion," Greenfield said without apology. "I'm interested in old buildings. Do you mind if I look around?"

She cleared her throat, found nothing to say, and wiped her hands on a dish towel while Greenfield wandered past two mammoth refrigerators and through a doorway in the far wall. There was nothing nineteenth-century about the kitchen furnishings: strip lighting, a bank of stainless-steel counters, aluminum racks hung with an army of pots, everything spare and functional. As Greenfield reappeared a door opened in the corner to one side of the long sink, and Julius came into the room.

He gaped at Greenfield, then at me, and finally at the girl. "Go take care of the bar for a few minutes, Ellie." She made a move toward the tray, but he put a hand on her arm and turned her toward the door. As she left he looked again at Greenfield, assuming a guileless smile that wouldn't have deceived a reeling drunk. "Any problem, Mr. Greenfield?"

"Where can we talk privately, Julius?"

Julius waved hospitably at several unpainted wooden stools scattered along a work counter. "This is fine."

Greenfield sat, resting one elbow on the counter. Julius waited for me to do the same, but I shook my head and stayed where I was, holding up the wall, despite Greenfield's unmistakably prompting glance. A small stab at rebellion. Julius apparently was not going to sit while I stood, and Greenfield had to make the best of it. He addressed the linoleum on the floor.

"You've heard about the woman who was found today in the stream at Hunegger?"

"Sure. It was on the news."

"She'd been missing since Tuesday night." He looked

up, but Julius had no comment to make. "It's possible she spent at least one of those nights in this hotel."

"*Here?*" Julius looked genuinely shocked. He shook his head decisively. "No way. The only woman who checked in since Tuesday was about seventy years old. She was with her husband, they were on their way to Buffalo."

"Mrs. Dakin would not have been a paying guest. Possibly you didn't even know she was here."

"She *snuck* in? How could she do that?"

Greenfield's hand, palm up, gestured to the doorway through which he'd gone earlier, and, presumably, discovered the back door.

"That's crazy. That door is locked, unless we're expecting deliveries. She couldn't get into a room anyway, without a key."

"She could, if she came by invitation."

Julius looked blank, then intrigued. "You mean she went up to some guy's room?" He was disarmed now, mentally reviewing his guests. "I guess she could have. It's hard to believe, with the single men I've got staying here. All three of them look as though TV and a cigar is about all the excitement they can take. And I got the impression *she* wasn't exactly . . . of course, you can never tell . . ."

"No, I don't think she was visiting a man. I think she was brought here by another woman. A woman who was staying in one of your rooms. Someone who wasn't registered."

"Not registered? How could—"

Silence fell with a crash, and reverberated. The room fell into a pocket of stillness. Even the refrigerator stopped whirring. Out in the bar someone laughed. Julius's face turned apple-red, then slowly paled. Greenfield held his eyes and said nothing, but Julius, inwardly searching for a smoke screen, found indignation.

"Listen, whoever I've got in these rooms is my business, Mr. Greenfield. I don't know what you're getting at. I don't understand this."

"This woman," Greenfield insisted quietly, "who wasn't registered—"

"That's personal! It's my personal business! What are you doing here? I don't like this kind of thing!"

"I have no interest in your private affairs," Greenfield said quietly, "except as they relate to a matter of importance to me."

"To *you!* Why should my business be important to *you?*"

"You're in no position to see any connection between the two, and I'll be as happy as you if there isn't any, but I have to be convinced of that. There's a good deal at stake. I'd be grateful if you'd tell me about Mrs. Byrnes."

Julius yelped at the name. Actually yelped. He turned his back on Greenfield, then turned around again, and sputtered, "This is really something! A man comes in off the street and knows all about my family! Where do you get your information?" He glared at Greenfield, at me, at Greenfield again, then leaned forward aggressively. "Did *he* send you here?"

Very slowly Greenfield said, "No one, Julius, sends me anywhere. I'm not in anyone's employ." He stood up and began to pace the length of the kitchen. "Frankly, if I'm right about what Mrs. Byrnes has been up to, you've been put in a very vulnerable position and it can't do you anything but good to have me on your side."

"My side is the same as hers!"

"But you didn't know she had a visitor."

"What visitor! Why do you keep dragging in this dead . . ." He broke off and swung his head slowly from side to side, a man of suddenly enlightened tolerance. "No. No, I don't know what you've got to do with this woman they found, maybe you're a private investigator, I'm not asking, but you're on the wrong track." His forearms on the counter, he leaned over them, confidential now. "Look, she came to me for help, who else would she go to, I'm her brother. I don't come between a man and his wife, that's for them to settle, but she's my sister and she needed some rest, she had to think things out. She needed a place to be alone once in a while. Sometimes she uses the room, sometimes not."

"She has a marital problem?"

Julius nodded. "Nothing to do with anything else."

"I gather it's fairly serious."

"Serious to her. She's got one husband, one kid, that's her life."

"And something was threatening that life. Or someone."

Julius turned over a hand. "I'm not going to discuss her problems with strangers. I can only tell you that woman they found had nothing to do with my sister's problems. Believe me, I'd know. She'd tell me. You're looking in the wrong place."

Greenfield nodded, his eyes on the floor. "That's possible." He wandered over to where the tray with the coffee pot and covered dish stood losing heat at one end of the counter. "But people have been known to behave uncharacteristically under stress. Mrs. Byrnes may have taken risks she kept to herself." He reached out and moved the coffee pot a fraction. "I'd have to hear it from her to believe it."

Julius inserted himself between Greenfield and the tray. "You have to have a pretty good reason to snoop around in people's private business, Mr. Greenfield. So far I don't know what your reason is, I never saw you before the other day, you could be anybody. I'm trying to protect my sister, she's in a very nervous state, and I have work to do. So forgive me, if you don't mind, I'd like you to go back to the front of the building now, this is really not a place for guests."

Greenfield stood looking at him for a while, quite detached, as though Julius were an illustration of some anthropological principle, then he started for the backstairs. "If you want to protect your sister, Julius, I suggest you get her to speak to you more frankly than she has." He went up the stairs.

Julius spared me one disillusioned glance before I left. I was his first female Judas.

At Greenfield's heels as he prowled, bemused, along the upstairs corridor, I voiced my incredulity in a subdued squeal, mindful of the doors we were passing, "*Connie?*"

"A desperate woman," he murmured, his thoughts already elsewhere, "Trouble at home. Marriage in jeopardy. A frantic scheme. A family hotel available with at least one empty room among twenty. Julius gives her a key—and there's the hiding place to carry out her plot."

"That dithering woman?" I squawked—in an undertone—"That Northeastern Southern belle? Planned and carried out an abduction of one of her own kind, just to throw suspicion on the camp? And then dumped the body in the stream? She can't even keep track of her own belongings in the ladies' room."

"Possibly she defies a scientific principle," he said, rummaging for his door key, "like the bumblebee." He opened the door and went in.

"Impossible," I insisted. "Out of the question. Connie Byrnes wouldn't have the self-confidence to invite Dakin for coffee, much less abduct her."

"I could be wrong. I'd prefer to be." He lit the lamp on the dresser.

My mind could only assimilate one impossibility at a time: it was too busy with the absurdity of knit-and-pearls as a counterinsurgent to absorb Greenfield's unprecedented suggestion that he could be wrong.

"Not to mention the motive." I sat on the edge of the bed. "It's a pretty thin motive, Charlie. Even assuming she's been planning her daughter's wedding in detail for twenty years and thinks it's about to be ruined by the camp's demonstration. Even assuming those nightmares she had were crawling with violent antinuclear protesters descending on the wedding reception, brickbats in hand, sweeping the engraved matchboxes off the tables, decimating the flower arrangements, tramping over the dance floor in their dirty sneakers—"

"I said a *marriage* in jeopardy, not a wedding." He moved to the window. "Very shortly"—he looked out at his favorite view—"Julius is going to deliver that tray to some room on this floor or the one above. It's unfortunate this place was designed to thwart covert surveillance."

"Unfortunate? To me it's irrelevant. I wouldn't know what we hoped to learn by it anyway. I'm not privy to the more esoteric aspects of this situation."

No reply. I glanced at my watch.

"Charlie, it's late, I have to get back to the camp. I'm due on patrol. I've done your bidding all day, come and gone at your behest, lost the only admirer I have in this neck of the woods, and I am not going to leave here in ignorance of vital information. What was that phone call all about, and while we're at it, I must have misheard, but a little while ago I *thought* you said, 'I'd *prefer* to be wrong.' What, for heaven's sake, does *that* mean?"

He left the window, sank into the fat chintz-covered chair, and sat there in the shadows, wrestling silently with something even he, apparently, was at a loss to articulate. I will write to the *Times*, I thought, this must not go unrecorded.

Eventually he stretched out his long legs, crossed them at the ankles, and said in deliberate and faintly sardonic accents, "There are those who believe there is a Supreme Being. Some Ultimate Consciousness, some Omnipotence. If there is, and if you consider a human life as a work of literature, then the Omnipotence who created that work has a lot to learn about narration. . . . The material is poorly organized. It rambles, it has extraneous clauses, it's repetitious. And any professional could have told the Omnipotence that the only satisfactory penultimate chapter to a life should be one that finally allows a man to turn his back on rampant imbecility and dementia. Five decades of slings and arrows may be necessary to sharpen the human faculty for making distinctions: beyond that it's not only sadistic, it's dull. . . . The windup should deliver something novel. . . . The experience, for instance, of unchallenged delight." He ran a hand slowly over his face. "But of course an Omnipotence won't put up with editing."

I waited. "Is that," I asked finally, "supposed to be an answer to my question?"

"Yes."

I stood up. "I'm going to be very busy all day tomorrow, because we'll be marching. Tomorrow night I'm going to rest. And Sunday I'm going home. So unless you can tell me something that doesn't require a glossary, I'll see you in the office, whenever you get there."

"I'm not impressed by attempts at intimidation."

I shrugged. "It's all I've got. *You* took the divining rod."

"Sit down."

I didn't, but I stayed put.

"The phone call I made at the gas station was to the home of Lieutenant Colonel Harwood. I asked him to get me some information. He got it and called me back. It seems"—his voice became carefully matter-of-fact—"that Frank Byrnes is a security guard at the base, and his hours are four P.M. to midnight."

CHAPTER SEVENTEEN

IT WAS A LITTLE BEFORE TWO IN THE MORNING. I patrolled the back meadow in the rain, sloshing around in rubber boots a size too large borrowed from Doris, water dripping onto my face from the hood of my slicker, oblivious of my surroundings, indifferent to my immediate responsibility, my mind racing wildly through the explosion of facts, times, places, people and possibilities detonated by Greenfield's revelation. The camp could have caught fire, I would have tramped, preoccupied, through the flames. The B52s could have taken off over my head with their lethal load, I wouldn't have spared them a glance. I had personal business to unravel, and as any observer of average human behavior will testify, personal business takes precedence over the threat of mass destruction any day.

Heath-Morecomb and the security guard!

Incredible! Unimaginable! Passionate activism, military commitment. Opposite sides of the fence. Literally. And they'd broken through that fence? Or dissolved it? Or even found it aphrodisiac? Good God, was it possible?

Yes, of course it was possible. Not only possible, classic. Impossible attractions have been immortalized in song and story. Historical examples probably number in the thousands.

As soon as I opened the door to possibility, a dozen recollections swam in to reinforce it.

His face, watching her as she played.

His voice, on the base that Tuesday night when he snapped on the flexicuffs, possibly familiar because I'd heard it only that afternoon, about three, under the willow tree.

H.M. coming and going through the woods in the dead of night, always at the same spot, where she'd trampled a path to the stream and possibly the willow tree, with her midnight trysts. *"His hours are four P.M. to midnight."*

Lynette at the gas station. "Dad's really moody these days."

Connie pictured in the *Ledger* at the gate on Friday, while the violin played, standing where she could see him watching her, see the band on the hat.

And the band was still there on Monday night. (But later H.-M. would have gone again to the willow tree.)

And on Tuesday afternoon the band was gone.

And on Thursday morning it was found in Dakin's car.

And on Thursday night H.-M. entered the woods again, with purpose. *(Frank, for God's sake, the police have my hatband, the one I gave you as a keepsake! How did that happen?)*

And two hours later Connie was hauled out of bed. "Keep your hands out of my pockets!"

And last night Frank Byrnes, the lawkeeper, finding himself with a criminal for a wife, stood behind the fence, his face torn with private pain. Assuming that particular guard was actually Frank Byrnes; there were a good number of guards behind the fence from 4:00 P.M. to midnight.

No. No way to ignore the weight of accumulated incidents. That guard was Byrnes.

All right; it was Byrnes, and the scenario was possible. Even probable. It was the consequences that didn't make sense. That Connie could have known about them, I accepted. That she would long to destroy the woman was more than plausible. That she could hatch such a devious scheme was not, I supposed, unthinkable. But beyond that, reason shook its head. How could a woman like Connie Byrnes outmaneuver such a woman as Alice Dakin? And why on earth would she kill her?

I trudged on, blinking the rain out of my eyes. Damn Lotte and her predictions, we *would* be marching in the rain. This was Saturday. Lynette's wedding day. I passed my fellow patroller, a woman called Edie from Charleston, a frail flower of Southern womanhood who had marched in demonstrations from Montgomery to Bismarck. There were two of us to a meadow tonight, security doubled, what with the march coming up and the discovery of Dakin's body. The police, Brenda said, had been around with more questions. The camp was nervous. It quivered. Lights had been burning in the barn long after midnight. I'd seen Doris crossing the field only half an hour before, and JoAnne a little before that. And Lotte in the kitchen shack with a flashlight.

I hadn't seen *her*. But she could hardly be under the willow tree tonight. In the burned-out house, perhaps. With her tape deck.

Two o'clock. I went to wake up my relief. The dawn patrol was being done in two shifts, potential marchers being in need of minimal rest. I tugged at a long, silky braid of hair in the darkness of a tent. "Time," I murmured, squelched to my own tent, crawled in, dripping rain on the blanket, and in no time at all lay there wide awake, raging at Heath-Morecomb.

If all this was true, she'd been acquiring Byrnes at the

same time she was annexing Greenfield! What was she, a conspicuous consumer? A collector? A scalp hunter? An addict? It was, of course, a sweet revenge. Greenfield deserved it. On the other hand, how *dare* she hurt him!

I reminded myself that the Byrnes affair was still speculation, still remained to be confirmed, no one had proclaimed it, there was no proof, no—as they say—hard evidence. Just a sneaking, intuitive, miserable certainty.

Ultimately I slept, and woke at eight to the crash and clatter of preparation for the march.

The rain had stopped. Lumpy pillows of cloud roamed around an uncertain sky. With any luck, poor Lotte would be deprived of the need for stoicism. I joined the noisy turmoil of to-ing and fro-ing, of banners, balloons, signs, badges, marching-order instructions, suggestions and countersuggestions, shouts, whistles, calls for order, coagulations of groups: Vermont Women's Action Corps, Pentagon Protest Group, New York Peace Coalition, Concerned Citizens, Minnesota Women for Peace, West Virginia Peace Alliance, International Antinuclear Offensive, Mothers Against Bombs, Boston Peace and Freedom Front, Survival, Inc. . . . Doris was meeting with the Peacekeepers, handpicked to arbitrate in the event of sticky situations, JoAnne was explaining the march route with the aid of a large diagram, Lotte was issuing orders to the group leaders, Heath-Morecomb . . . Heath-Morecomb stood on an empty crate, two feet above the milling throng, organizing the separation of chanters and singers.

Brenda was running back and forth between the action and the wash-house, looking pale. "I've got my fucking *period!*"

At ten minutes to ten I found myself clutching one-tenth of the top edge of a twenty-foot blue banner showing a mushroom cloud with the message in foot-high white letters: THERE'S NO LIBERTY WHERE THERE'S NO LIFE. Ten abreast, we were to carry it before us until we dropped or the fingers went numb, whichever came first. At five minutes to ten I heard my name shouted and a young woman told me I was wanted on the phone in the office. I beat my zigzag way through to the barn.

Greenfield's voice came broodingly over the wire. "I've checked out of the hotel."

"Checked—! Why?"

"My departure was requested. Mrs. Byrnes has bolted and I'm being blamed. Julius came pounding on my door at midnight, thinking I'd bound her to a chair and was grilling her. At any rate, she's gone."

"Gone where? Not home, for sure." And if she was hiding from—her husband—she wouldn't go to Ethel Sprague's house. That would be the first place he'd look.

"Wherever she went, Julius couldn't find her. Apparently she didn't seek refuge with another member of the extensive family."

There was the sound, from outside, of chanting, and of several hundred feet hitting the ground simultaneously.

"Charlie, they're marching, where are you going?"

"I'll be at the only place I can think of that would be a magnet for Mrs. Byrnes."

". . . Oh. Right. Well, you know where *I'll* be."

I ran out of the barn, saw the blue banner among the bobbing heads turning out of the campgrounds onto the road, caught up with it and retrieved my twenty inches of canvas. There'd been a change of personnel in my absence, but it was a full minute before I realized the hands holding the adjacent twenty inches belonged to Heath-Morecomb. I kept my eyes firmly fixed on the rows of heads in front of me, among them, Brenda's. Holding a sign with one hand and her stomach with the other, she marched and chanted.

We were heading for Hunegger, on a long circular route that would traverse the length of Padua and double back along the base perimeter to the gate. All of us a little nervous, wondering if and where the counterdemonstrators would strike and how many. In twenty minutes we were crossing the small iron bridge over the stream at Hunegger. Marching over Dakin's grave, I thought with a shudder. There was a deputy sheriff standing alongside his patrol car, and another farther up the block, but this time it was because of us. No need, a few dozen local residents were scattered along either side of the road, but they were passive, merely watching.

We marched along without incident, across the abandoned railroad line and into Padua, chanters, singers, banners, balloons and all. Made a brief detour, one block square, to pass within sight of the hospital where Harriet was slowly recovering, all arms waving at the windows as we went by, the long caterpillar winding around the block and back to the route. My mind was busy with Connie Byrnes, mysteriously decamped. Why? Had Julius, when he'd taken up the tray, asked uncomfortable questions? Told her about Greenfield's suspicions and sent her into a panic? Would she panic if she was innocent? And where had she gone? Where *could* she go, at that hour, if not home, nor to Ethel's, nor to family? The Sycamore? How would she get there? She had no car. Taxis were scarce, and had to be called, and the only phone at the Plaza was in the bar. Had she *walked* somewhere? A sudden image of the woman in the bridal shop. "The mother is wearing peach taffeta . . . shoes dyed to match . . . feet so swollen she couldn't get into them."

Connie Byrnes, on swollen feet, trudging along the dark Padua streets at midnight, fearful, desolate, about to lose her daughter, having already lost her husband. Connie, who probably didn't know a cantata from an oratorio and didn't care. What was Bach or Bizet to her. . . .

Had it really happened? I turned to look at Heath-Morecomb. She marched with flair, of course, head thrown back, aureole of copper hair blazing, chin thrust forward, her face bright with defiance like an unpopular sovereign braving the rabble.

We turned onto the boulevard. There were people here, quite a few, standing and watching.

"What is it, Maggie, are you committing me to memory?"

Well, go on, all of life is chance.

"I was wondering if you cared for opera," I said.

"Mad about it."

"Charlie once called it the triumph of agitated music over puerile drama."

"That's a pity."

"I found your tape of *Carmen.*"

"Ah! I wondered where it had got to."

"I thought you might have been consulting it for pointers."

"*Pointers?* What are you hinting at? Don't hint."

"Frank Byrnes."

Eyes straight ahead. We marched another half block. She looked angry.

"Why should you spy on *me,* for God's sake?"

"It came to light. In the course of events. There *have* been events."

"What nonsense."

We marched on.

"Pointers. I don't need *pointers. Certainly* I was being seductive. In the most *general* sense. It's why I'm here. To win people over. To turn them around. The rest simply— evolved." A smile crept over her face, both mischievous and gentle. "I happened to see him watching me. Noticed his eyes, saw him move, heard him laugh. It's a wonderful laugh. . . . Beware the beguiled, they do their own beguiling." She gave me a sidelong glance. "You mentioned this to Charlie?"

"No. He suggested it to me."

"Bloody hell."

For a woman with her hand caught in the cookie jar, she looked singularly unabashed. If a touch melancholy.

Well, now I knew. Now it was no longer circumstantial evidence. And all that time it hadn't even occurred to me. All those signs and portents had passed me by. Yet Greenfield had headed for it like a homing pigeon. Arrived at it, no doubt, by the same route as Connie. Via viscera.

We were approaching the stretch of boulevard along which I'd followed JoAnne's car to the corner where the big white church stood so comfortably behind its luxurious lawn. All aflutter now, I supposed, with bridesmaids and nosegays? *The bride, in white lace over peau de soie, came down the aisle on the arm of her haggard father. The mother of the bride was absent in peach taffeta. The wedding was attended by nervous relatives, including her uncle Julius.*

A block to the left, the buff-colored brick of the new apartment complex rose above the low roofs of the boulevard. It came to me suddenly where Connie Byrnes had gone in the middle of the night. *"Those new apartments are really neat—you know my mother, she wants it all fixed up before we see it, we don't even get the key until after the wedding."* Slept on the floor, most likely, so as not to sully the chaste furniture. Slept within blocks of the church.

The church? But there had to be more than one church in Padua! Had Greenfield checked to be certain he had the right one?

There were crowds, now, lining the streets. Police were out in force. Insults were being hurled. Only insults, so far. We were in sight of the church when I sensed the procession slowing down. There was a great deal of shouting up ahead, flags waving. Uniforms from the boulevard behind us began to move up toward the head of the procession, urging the crowds back from the road. Abruptly the group ahead of us came to a standstill, and we stopped behind them. JoAnne appeared from a group toward the back, fighting her way to the front. Heath-Morecomb let go of the banner and went after her. Word filtered back: Confrontation. A crowd of three hundred flag-wavers was blocking the street. Four Hundred. Five. It was the Dakin counterdemonstration. No, it was the townspeople. The police were asking us to disperse. No, they were asking the flag-wavers to disperse. They were asking *everybody* to disperse. (I could just imagine Doris dispersing. "You see this permit? This is a permit to march!" Framed. In triplicate.)

The people on the sidelines began to mill forward, not wanting to miss the action. They spilled into the roadway, jostling us. One of our signs went down, underfoot, got trampled. Arguments erupted. In seconds a hundred balloons rose into the air. "Peace," "Life," "No Nukes" went floating, red, white and blue, over the bobbing heads. Townspeople jumped up, grabbing for them. I felt the banner rip as we were pushed in opposite directions. "Fold it!" I heard myself shout, and began to gather up the banner from the near end. I saw Brenda push her way to the side of the road, holding her sign high, saw Mariko craning her head, trying to see beyond the giants surrounding her, saw a bizarre figure in peach taffeta struggling against the tide, trying to cross the street.

Connie!

Trying to beat her way through our ranks with a peach-colored shoe in her hand!

I stuffed the banner into somebody's arms, elbowed my way through the chaos, grabbed a peach taffeta arm. The shoe landed on the side of my head. Her made-up face was expressionless, her eyes blank, wisps of dark hair straggled down her forehead from the curled coiffure. She flailed, without anger, as though she were fighting a river current. She wanted only to reach the other side, where the church stood.

"Mrs. Byrnes!" I shouted. "Come with me! This way!"

I dragged her back through the crowd, and she resisted, striking out with the shoe, but she was at a disadvantage on her uneven feet. Pushing and pressing and shouldering, Connie's shoe pummeling my back, I made it to where Brenda was leaning limply against the wall of a building.

"Urgent!" I said in her ear, clutching Connie's wrist with both hands. "You know what Greenfield looks like? The man at the Plaza! The room with the shower! He's sitting in a tan Plymouth somewhere around that church across the street. Find him and tell him to drive around behind the crowd and come into—into"—I looked at the sign on the cross street—"Cypress Avenue! Tell him I've got her!"

She looked at me with the dazed look of a battle casualty conscripted into a dance marathon.

"Fast, Brenda! Now!" I carved a path up the sidewalk and into Cypress Avenue. "I'm taking you to the church, Mrs. Byrnes. Around the block. It's easier. You can't make it through that crowd. They'll tear your dress."

She was still pulling back, but without conviction, her resistance and her makeup both wilting as she limped and hobbled after me. I stopped in front of a large brown house set back from the road. On the boulevard, I could see Doris talking to the police while the camp peacekeepers tried to establish détente with the bellowing mob of flag-wavers. Reporters with their mini-cams jockeyed for position. Michael and his equipment appeared at the corner, and he scrambled barefoot onto the hood of a car parked on Cypress.

Connie was a weight on my hand. "Do you want to put on your shoe?"

She was breathing heavily. She looked at the shoe. She looked at her swollen foot. She looked at me. "I'm late. I'll be late."

"I'm going to give you a lift. There's a car coming." I *hope* there's a car coming. "Can you make it to the next corner?"

She began to limp up the street.

"I—can do anything. I can do anything. I'm her *mother*. I arranged everything. Seventy-five people. The orchestra. How would it look—if I didn't show up. I have my rights. Nobody's going to—walk all over me. . . ."

We were almost at the corner when the Plymouth turned into Cypress Avenue and came to a stop. I opened the back door and Connie pulled instinctively against my hand, then sagged against the car, then got in as though she'd ordered a limousine. I sat beside her, reached over and locked her door and then mine. Greenfield made a U-turn, drove back around the corner and up a street that ran parallel to the boulevard, then on until we came to a kind of pocket park—a handful of benches, several triangles of grass and a fountain. Deserted. Everyone was on the boulevard, watching or warring.

"Please drive faster," Connie said, "I'm going to be late."

Greenfield pulled into the curb next to the park, and stopped.

"Mrs. Byrnes," he said, "I've been staying at the Plaza Hotel. I happened to see you going into your room, late last Tuesday night, with a woman who—"

She lunged for the door. I grabbed her arm. She wailed. A piercing, bone-chilling sound, a baying, the hound of the Baskervilles. She keened, she howled, she curled up on the seat and rocked back and forth. Greenfield rolled up the windows, rested his elbow on the steering wheel and sat there with his head in his hand.

Finally he turned and shouted at her, "Police!"

She flinched as though he'd slapped her. Her mouth stayed open, but silent.

"If you don't want the police here," he said soothingly, "just explain what the woman was doing in your room. Quietly."

She leaned forward, whispering urgently, "It wasn't my fault, I didn't know, how could I know, it wasn't—"

"Know what, Mrs. Byrnes?"

"That she wouldn't . . . that she . . ." She closed her mouth tightly, her lips disappearing, her body shaking with silent sobs.

"Just tell me why Alice Dakin was in your room."

She took a shuddering breath, staring at him. Greenfield looked at his watch. "It's getting late—"

She poured it out in a rush, still whispering, leaning forward, trembling visibly, her hands clutching the back of the driver's seat. "I went to the base with some other women their husbands were on the bowling team, and

205

later when they were going home I said I'd wait for Frank and when everybody was gone I waited near the bushes, near the house where Mrs. Dakin was visiting. I knew she'd be there Ethel told me, and when she was driving down the road I waved at her, I said Mrs. Dakin you remember me Connie Byrnes I'm a friend of Ethel Sprague, I said could you give me a lift into Padua and she took me, all the way in the car I was thinking how can I say it, we got to the hotel I said Mrs. Dakin I have something important to tell you about those people at the peace camp would you come up to my room for a minute, she said tell me here but I wanted to get her up to the room before my brother closed the bar and came in to check the kitchen, I said no I have to show you something, it's up there, it was in my bag but I said it was up there, she said no she had a headache, I said it won't take long, please, we went up to the room, she said do you have any aspirin, I knew I didn't but I had sleeping pills because I haven't been sleeping well they help me when I have a headache, if I only take one it doesn't put me to sleep just gets rid of the headache they're very mild, so I gave her one I didn't tell her what it was, then I said Mrs. Dakin I have an idea I know a way to ruin those people at the peace camp and I told her how she could pretend to be kidnapped, and just stay in my room and not tell anybody where she was, and I would put something in the car so they'd suspect the camp and give them a bad name so they'd have to shut down, and I showed her the—the thing from that woman's hat, she said no, no she couldn't be a party to anything like that then she went into the bathroom, when she came out she said she didn't feel well I said lie down on the bed, I sat in the chair she fell asleep really fast asleep and I looked at her sleeping there and I thought how could she refuse to do it, it was perfect it was the perfect way to get the camp why couldn't she see that, how could she ruin everything, all my plans, I was counting on it, counting on it, it was the only way to get rid of that, that person, it was the only way to save my life, it

206

was so important, so important, I planned it so carefully, it took so long I had to think and think and now she was going to ruin everything, just saying no she couldn't be a party, just like that, that was terrible she had to do it she had to, it was too much, the wedding and Frank, Frank, what would I do where would I go, why couldn't she just lie there and sleep and let me go ahead with it she didn't even have to do anything, just not go back to the Sycamore, just not go back and I'd do all the rest, I'd take all the chances, all she had to do was stay in the room, stay in the room, why couldn't she just stay in the room, she was sleeping with her head on a pillow there was another pillow beside her I picked it up and put it on her face so she would stay in the room and not wake up and go back to the Sycamore, I held the pillow on her face and then I took her car keys out of her bag and I drove to Hunegger and left the car there and the thing from the hat, I walked back, it took so long and I got blisters, I called home and said I was staying at Ethel's he didn't care and I sat in the chair all night I was afraid to sleep, and she was lying there on the bed I didn't know what to do and then it was morning and I sat in the room all day I didn't let anybody in, when it was dark I went out the back, I called Ethel we put her in the stream but it wasn't my fault I just wanted her to stay in the *room!*"

We sat there listening to her pant until Greenfield rolled down the windows and turned back to her. "Where," he asked softly, "did you get that hatband you left in Mrs. Dakin's car?"

Her mouth quivered. Her eyes welled.

"Did you take it off the hat?"

"I—wouldn't—*touch*—her hat."

"Did you find it in your home?"

She sobbed. "In—my home. In *my—home*. I wish—I could have—put the—pillow on—*her* face!"

Greenfield turned back to the steering wheel. Eventually he started the car, drove to within half a block of the church, told me to keep her there while he got her an escort, went off toward the church and returned with Julius, who looked as though he were fighting a five-alarm fire singlehanded as he half carried his sister away, knowing he could no longer protect her.

I wondered if Greenfield, in the church, had come face-to-face with Frank Byrnes.

CHAPTER EIGHTEEN

"How LONG IS CHARLES GOING TO STAY IN Marlboro?" Elliot asked.

"He didn't say." I put the remains of the lemon chicken and wild rice in the refrigerator, ate the last stalk of asparagus, turned on the dishwasher. "I'm going to take a shower."

"You took one before dinner."

"That was two hours ago." I gave him a grin. He gave an indulgent grimace. On my way through the living room I picked up the clipping I'd cut out of that morning's *Times:* ANTINUCLEAR PROTESTERS MARCH UPSTATE *Padua, N.Y. Forty-six women from the Hunegger peace camp and three local residents were arrested on Saturday during a march protesting the presence of Cruise missiles at Hunegger Air Force Base. When a confrontation devel-*

oped between the marchers and a group of local residents blocking the road, County Sheriff Raymond Slater was unsuccessful in his attempt to disperse the obstructing residents and directed the marchers to detour by way of an adjacent road. Those that refused were placed in trucks and removed for arraignment. The three local residents arrested with the women had joined the protesters as a gesture of support. "They have a right to march," said Beatrice Vigler, one of the three arrested.

I stepped into the shower, wondering if I was making up for lost time or emulating Lady Macbeth: my own efforts to nail Heath-Morecomb hadn't been so different from Connie's. I had well and truly flung my winter garment of content into the crazy fires of spring.

That hatband. Not kitsch, after all, but an acronym. Britons Against Nuclear Disaster.

The last I'd seen of Heath-Morecomb had been the night before, when I took a valedictory walk around the back meadow and heard the sound of music from the burned-out house. I'd found her sitting on the step of the rickety porch, peering up at the stars, Brahms' Third Symphony issuing in its incomparable, haunting splendor from her portable tape machine. Her voice was husky when she spoke. "Do you realize," she said softly, "that the minute those missiles are launched, *Brahms*"—reverently touching the source of the music—"will no longer exist?"

I stood in the dark, unable to speak.

Finally I went back to my tent, thinking yes, and if it weren't for the missiles, Heath-Morecomb would have been in England, Dakin would have been in Idaho and Connie would have been at home and not needed sleeping pills. Missiles, apparently, didn't have to be launched to cause havoc, they only had to exist.

It was the end of the week before Greenfield called to say he was in the office. I drove down Poplar Avenue, parked in front of the old three-story white frame house and went up the path to the narrow porch. My hand on the doorknob, I hesitated. If I hear that same violin concerto coming from the stereo, I thought, I'm resigning. I opened the door: César Franck. I went up the narrow stairway. Greenfield was in the swivel chair sorting through the piled-up mail. I watched him anxiously, wondering how deeply the H.-M. episode had cut.

He glanced up. "Why are you looking at me like a hospital nurse?"

"Just wondering if you're healing properly."

He slit open an envelope, scanned the contents, tossed them in the wastebasket. "A journalist," he paraphrased, "can survive anything but a misspelled byline."

I relaxed: it hadn't been fatal. And maybe we'd get some work done, now that he was back to normal. Helen and Calli would be relieved, when they came in on Monday, to see that he'd recovered from his spell of temporary insanity.

He leaned back in the swivel chair—an E flat squeak—and looked up from under the eyebrows. "Now that you're back to normal, Maggie," he said, "we might be able to get some work done. The last time you were in this office you seemed to be going through a spell of temporary insanity."

On a hot Thursday evening in mid-July my telephone rang. The voice was unmistakable.

"I'm home," Brenda said. "Listen, you know about dogs. I met these people who want to get rid of a dog. What do you think? Should I take him? You think it's crazy to keep a dog in a fifth-floor walkup?"

"What kind of dog is it?"

"I think it's a Great Pyrenees."

About the Author

LUCILLE KALLEN is the author of the first feminist comic novel, OUTSIDE THERE, SOMEWHERE, as well as INTRODUCING C.B. GREENFIELD, an American Book Award nominee, C.B. GREENFIELD: THE TANGLEWOOD MURDER, C.B. GREENFIELD: NO LADY IN THE HOUSE, and C.B. GREENFIELD: THE PIANO BIRD (all published by Ballantine). She has written for television (including the acclaimed series "Your Show of Shows") and for the theater.